I0737326

MARY CRAWFORD

Love AND Injustice

HIDDEN HEARTS
PROTECTION UNIT BOOK 1

COPYRIGHT

Published on December 1, 2018, by Diversity Ink Press and Mary Crawford. Author may be reached at MaryCrawfordAuthor.com.

ISBN-978-1-945637-27-8 • ASIN: B07HDJPLN3

Cover Design: CoverBound.com

Hidden Beauty Series

Until the Stars Fall from the Sky
So the Heart Can Dance
Joy and Tiers
Love Naturally
Love Seasoned
Love Claimed
If You Knew Me (and other silent musings) (novella)
Jude's Song
The Price of Freedom (novella)
Paths Not Taken
Dreams Change (novella)
Heart Wish (100% charity release)
Tempting Fate
The Letter
The Power of Will

HIDDEN HEARTS SERIES

Identity of the Heart
Sheltered Hearts
Hearts of Jade
Port in the Storm (novella)
Love is More Than Skin Deep
Tough
Rectify
Pieces (a crossover novel)
Hearts Set Free
Freedom (a crossover novel)
The Long Road to Love (novella)
Love and Injustice (Protection Unit)
Out of Thin Air (Protection Unit)
Soul Scars (Protection Unit)

OTHER WORKS:
The Power of Dictation
Vision of the Heart
#AmWriting: A Collection of Letters to Benefit The
Wayne Foundation

Dedication

To those who serve the greater good
without thanks or recognition –

We honor you.

Chapter One

Cody

I stir some more sugar and cream into my coffee since my former partner, Dylan, isn't around to razz me about it, and look over at my breakfast companion who is contentedly drinking his straight black. "So, how is your sister? It's been years now, but she was still one of the best rookie cop I ever trained."

John grins. "Yeah, my sister is a talented little spitfire — but if Tayanita is right, she might not be little for long." John's face is lit up with mirth.

"How's that?" I ask, playing along, curious about what my friend thinks is so amusing about the woman I trained during her rookie year as a cop.

"My wife has a hunch Katie might be pregnant, so I guess things are going okay with Logan."

"Is Tayanita picking up the same sort of sixth sense Ketki has?" I tease.

John throws back his head and laughs. "No, I think this is related to all of Nita's experience as a nurse. Katie is in a bit of shock. Apparently, they didn't think this was even possible because of the injuries Logan sustained while he was in the military."

I jump when someone clears his throat right next to my ear. I look up and notice Dashonte standing next to me. "Hey, long time no see. How is college?"

"I'm off for the summer, but my chemistry class was a pain during spring term. I'm starting to second-guess my plan to become a vet."

"Doctor Stuart says you are a natural. Eventually, you'll get through the coursework, and then you can get to the fun part."

He clears his throat again. "Probably, but that's not really what I came to talk about."

Something about his tone makes me straighten up in my chair. "What's up? Do we need to talk privately?"

Dashonte looks down at Tuffy, John's guide dog and carefully maneuvers around him as he sits down. "Nah, Mr. Ashford is cool. He works at Identity Bank. That might come in handy."

John's eyebrows come together in a concerned expression. "You do know I don't work for the law enforcement side, right? I just help make gaming software more accessible for people with disabilities."

"Yeah, I know. Ketki brags about you all the time when she brings her cats into the vet clinic. But, you know the person in charge. Right now, that's good enough for me."

"So what's the problem?" John inquires.

Dashonte twists a paper napkin in front of him in knots as he tells me his story in a disjointed burst of speech. "My mom wouldn't want me to say anything to you, but it's about my little brother."

"What about him? Is he shoplifting again?" I ask. I take a sip of my coffee and notice it's already getting cold. I have a hunch it's going to be a long day.

"No, I wish that's all it was," Dashonte says with a sigh. "I can't find DeAndre."

"Your little brother, right?" I surmise.

"Yeah, no one has seen him in a couple days."

"He play video games?" John questions.

"A few. He's mostly into skateboarding and hanging out at the skate park."

"You've checked with all his buddies?" John asks.

Dashonte nods. "Multiple times. They're tired of me blowin' up their phones. Nobody's heard sh — um … nothing from him. I mean, usually he checks in with my mom around dinner time if he's not coming home — but for almost three days … nothing."

"You think he's hanging out with the wrong kids again?"

Dashonte bristles. "No man! I don't!"

My skepticism must've been clear on my face without me having to say a single word because Dashonte blows out a breath. "Look, I know you don't believe me — but DeAndre was completely freaked out when Tallulah Johnson went missing a few weeks ago. He had a huge crush on her. DeAndre was trying to work up the nerve to ask her out before she disappeared. When she went missing it shook him bad and he started paying attention to Ma's curfew. He even told her if no cops were available to patrol our neighborhood, he would have to grow up and be one."

"Wow! That's quite a turnaround," I mutter as I begin

taking notes in the notebook I constantly keep in my pocket. "What does your mom think of all this?"

"She doesn't know what to think. After all, she thought it would be my older brother who'd be in danger — you know, with him being stationed overseas as a Ranger and all. She never figured DeAndre would be the one in trouble. In her mind, he's still a little baby. I think part of her wants to believe he's not really missing. She's hoping he's hanging out with his buddies somewhere and simply hasn't called in."

I hold up my hand to stop him. "I mean, I hate to ask the obvious here, but have you tried to contact your brother on his phone?"

"Yeah, I've called so many times, his voicemail won't even take any more calls. I even had Daquan try. DeAndre always picks up for Daquan, but even he didn't have any luck."

I lift my pen up from my notebook as I look up at him. "Daquan?"

"My big brother, the Army Ranger. D-A-Q-U-A-N G-R-E-E-L-E-Y," he spells out slowly as he waits for me to write it down.

"Has your mom called the police?" John asks. "Your little brother is still a kid, right?"

Dashonte grimaces. "He doesn't like to think so — but yeah, he is. He's only sixteen. My mom doesn't want to get the police involved. You know, that doesn't always go so well in my neighborhood. Sometimes good people end up dead," he shrugs helplessly as he looks at me apologetically. "Sorry Officer Erickson, no disrespect intended, that's just how it is."

I place my hand on his shoulder. "I know what you

mean. I wish it wasn't true. I've been in the field long enough to know you're telling the truth. I understand your mom's concern. How long has your brother been gone?"

"At least two days, maybe three. I was out of town, so I wasn't around the first day, but my mom says she couldn't find him at his usual hangouts."

I close my notebook and tuck my pen in my pocket. "Okay, how about this? Why don't you go home and tell your mom we'd like to talk to her, informally at first? Maybe John can ask Tristan to come on board."

John nods. "Yep. It's more his thing than mine. Besides, I bet your mom already knows Tristan through neighborhood events."

"She does. Tristan came out and repaired some stuff in our apartment when our landlord wouldn't do anything. I guess he and Mitch do a bunch of stuff with Habitat for Humanity. My mom likes him a lot. She might be cool with that."

"Okay, you have my number, right?" I ask. I start to hand Dashonte a business card but he waves it off. He holds up his cell phone.

"Dude, I got it all in here. I'll text you."

"I hope it's merely a miscommunication and you find DeAndre soon. If you need anything, let me know."

Dashonte stuffs his phone in his pocket and walks away.

After a few moments John scrubs his hand down his face. "Is it just me, or does all this sound really familiar?"

A knot grows in the middle of my stomach. "I have a gut feeling, but I want to hear how it strikes you."

"Ever since Ketki worked on that sting with Savannah, I keep a close eye on stories involving teenagers. It seems as if there's a lot of bad stuff happening — more than is statistically normal. It makes me want to lock my daughter in the house and throw away the key."

"I don't know if it's all related or not — it's too early to tell. But, I know Dashonte's family is under a phenomenal amount of stress. DeAndre could be a runaway, trying to escape his problems. I know someone who could probably give us some perspective. Let me see if she'll talk to me."

John must've caught something in my tone because he quirks an eyebrow at me. "Sounds like there might be more to the story there."

"Oh, there is — but you probably don't have a week to hear it all."

"Why Detective Erickson, you look dashing today. Did you have to testify in court?" Crystal Downing greets as she comes to the counter. Her eyes sparkle, and she has a bright smile.

I blush, embarrassed to be busted by the friendly receptionist. "No, not today. Is Ms. Clarkson available, by any chance?" I adjust my tie and try not to fidget like a teenager who's about to ask a girl out for the first time.

Crystal lets out a small gasp and her smile fades. "Oh dear, you mean you haven't heard?" she whispers. "I thought everyone knew."

"Is Tori all right?" I ask as I try to interpret Crystal's

distraught expression.

Crystal mutely shakes her head as she digs through a box containing files on her desk. With shaking hands, she removes a piece of paper from a file. She clears her throat and reads in a monotone voice I've never heard her use. "Victoria Clarkson is no longer employed by the Prosecutor's Office in this county. We have no further comment in this office. Questions can be directed to the District Attorney, Derek Zane's office."

Crystal drops the paper like it's burning. She can barely stand to look at it as she tucks it back into the folder and puts the folder back in the plastic box.

When she looks back at me, she avoids my questioning glance. "You're kidding! Tori was just promoted to Assistant District Attorney. This stinks! You've been my friend since I was a rookie cop. You know I can't leave it at that. What's the real scoop?"

"I can't tell you, Cody. I'll lose my job. I can't believe you don't know. It's been all over the news. Have you been living under a rock?"

I scrub my hand down my face. "No, I just got back into town. My grandma died a little over a month ago."

"Oh, no! I'm so sorry," Crystal exclaims.

"Me too. It was a long time comin'. She'd been fighting emphysema for some time. In a way, it was a blessing. We just weren't expecting my grandfather to pass away a week later. My mom is simply devastated. So, I stayed with my parents a bit longer than I planned."

"Totally understandable. You're such a good man," Crystal says with a teary smile. "You're the type of person Tori needs in her life right now."

I clear my throat nervously. "That's nice of you to

say — but my relationship with Ms. Clarkson has always been somewhat complicated. We can never seem to get our timing quite right.”

Crystal shoots me a ghost of a smile. My mind is racing as I try to figure out how to interpret it. “Well … I wouldn't know anything about that, specifically … but I know a little about Tori's approach to timing. She's a stickler for her schedule — even when she is on 'vacation'. She likes the little kickboxing gym — you know, the one over by the aquatic center? It doesn't look like much. But … it's her favorite way to decompress. If I know anything about her, she's probably practically living there these days.”

I can't suppress my grin as I lean over the counter and give Crystal a brief hug. “Thank you. Next time I come, I'll bring you your favorite latte. The pumpkin spice is on me.”

“Mr. Erickson,” she calls after me as I leave the office. “It's only summer. I expect to see you way before pumpkin spice season, you hear?”

Chapter Two

Tori

"WHOA! THE LADIES TELL me I got a pretty face, so don't knock my teeth out, m'kay?" Anthony teases as he braces the heavy bag on his shoulder. His speech is slurred as he talks around his mouth guard.

"Sorry, I have a bunch of stuff on my mind. I wasn't paying attention to my form. Maybe I should call it a day," I admit, as I start to pull the athletic tape off my ankle.

Anthony spits out his bright orange mouth guard. "What's up? You're usually a total warrior." He grabs a towel and straddles a weight bench a few feet away from the sparring ring.

I slump down on the other end of the bench and turn around so he can take the kinesthetic tape off my shoulder.

"Let's just say life has been kicking me in the teeth lately. I knew it would be hard to take care of my mom. The doctors warned me, but I didn't know it would be this hard. I baked her a cake for her birthday — it was red velvet and everything. She threw it at me."

Anthony's eyes widen. "She threw a cake at you?

Why? When you brought cookies the other day, I didn't think they were awful. Maybe not Martha Stewart good, still they weren't bad —"

I sigh and wipe away tears with the back of my hand. "No, it doesn't have anything to do with my cooking — or at least I hope not. Yesterday, my mom had no idea who I was. She couldn't remember me at all. She thought I was trying to poison her. It didn't matter that she lives in my house with my graduation pictures on the wall with her standing right next to me. She has no idea who I am."

"No wonder you're off your game."

"I can't even blame my mom. Have you seen the way they've been talking about me in the paper? I don't know who they're talking about, but it's not me."

"You mean you didn't shag anybody in an elevator?"

"No! Eww!" I answer as a visceral shudder passes through my body.

"Rumor has it you gave the grateful defendant a blow job while he was in handcuffs — and maybe even more."

I whirl around and face Anthony with fire shooting from my eyes. "The rumor is dead wrong! I built a career prosecuting sex crime. Does that seem like something I would do?"

Anthony puts his hands up in front of his chest in a gesture of innocence. "Hey, don't shoot the messenger. I'm just repeating what I heard. I'm just sayin' maybe you did something to earn that reputation —"

Gritting my teeth, I narrow my eyes. I try to keep my voice as level as possible. "Oh, you mean like graduating in the top ten percent of my class and working my way through law school after working as a teacher for high-risk kids. You know, because I like to live my life on the edge like that."

My fitness coach looks uncomfortable as he responds, "No, I mean the way you dress."

I glance down at my hot pink T-shirt emblazoned with the phrase "Just do it", and my black yoga pants. When I meet his gaze with an incredulous look, I ask, "You do realize I don't wear this to court, right? I have perfectly respectable business suits. My business suits cost about as much as you make in a month."

"I know. I saw pictures of 'em on the news. They're nice and tight too."

I take the towel from around my neck and throw it at Anthony's chest. "It's too bad. You were a good trainer — but, I need someone who's on my team. I won't be back."

As I turn to leave, Anthony places his hand on my shoulder. "Wait, I didn't mean it like that —"

"Not much room for misunderstanding there." I respond as I duck out of his grasp. "Next time you might want to think before you talk."

Anthony looks up at the guy standing next to us and shrugs, obviously looking for backup and sympathy.

"Don't look at me," he responds. "Tori has a point."

It isn't until I hear a very familiar sexy voice that I realize Cody Erickson has probably overheard my whole humiliating, *very* personal conversation — as if I thought my crappy day couldn't get any worse.

Fortunately, Cody can't see the internal dialogue consisting of copious amounts of self-flagellation running through my mind when he reaches his hand out toward mine. "You look like you would rather be anywhere than here. Want to grab a cup of coffee?"

I pause for a moment. "Not really dressed for it."

"They don't care at Tough Breaks. It's kind of a come-as-you-are sort of joint."

Shaking my head, I stare down at the floor. "Nothing personal Cody, I'm not ready to face the public right now."

"I can work with that. Coffee to go works for me."

"Tori, you can't quit on me. You've got goals to reach —" Anthony argues.

Cody stares down Anthony. "I think Ms. Clarkson made it clear her goals have changed."

"He's right, Anthony. Lose my number. Permanently."

"Ahh, man! You're my best client. I didn't say anything to you that everyone else isn't saying."

"That's the problem. I expected better from you. I thought you respected me. I figured you were my friend. Although these days, I suppose I don't know who my friends are anymore."

"I don't know if that's exactly true," Cody murmurs in my ear as he places his hand in the small of my back and escorts me out of the gym with so much class it seems as if we're leaving a five-star restaurant.

"That's because you don't know the whole story," I mumble.

"Maybe not, but I know you."

With everything going on in my life right now, Cody's simple declaration is enough to make me sway on my feet and dissolve into tears.

The retro rack of stereo equipment in Cody's comfortable den makes me smile. It reminds me of the set up my dad used to play gospel and blues music after church when I was little. "Aretha Franklin, Etta or Nat King Cole?" Cody asks me as he turns on his stereo speakers.

"How did you know I'm a fan?"

Cody smiles as he studies me intently. "I've watched you dance at a charity ball or two. You seem to enjoy all music, but you really love the old stuff."

I'm a little startled at his observation. I know I've watched him over the years, but I didn't realize he reciprocated. "We've never danced together. Why is that?" I blurt.

He hands me my hot chocolate and croissant before sitting down and crossing his leg over his knee. "I don't know. I guess we could never get our timing right. When I was single, you were dating the Navy pilot. Whatever happened to him?"

I let out a burst of startled laughter. "Oh, you mean the guy who was more attached to his little black book than me? I took him to the airport and dropped him off. I changed my phone number and moved. I think he got the hint."

"Ouch! That's one way to send a message. I'm sorry I was so rude to you about him back then. I had no clue you were dealing with all that. It looked oh-so-perfect from the outside."

"Don't worry about it. Appearances can be

deceiving. What about you? Are you still dating the girl with the crazy laugh?" I stop short and cover my mouth with my hand. "Oops, I probably shouldn't have said anything. That was rude."

Cody throws his head back and laughs. "No, that's probably the nicest thing you could've said about Rainah."

"I take it that it didn't end well?" I ask after I sip my chocolate and take a bite of my croissant.

"It tends not to be a healthy relationship, when the only reason someone is dating you is to dig up dirt on you so she can get the case against her big brother overturned."

"Wow! I thought I was the only one whose life was completely crazy."

"I've heard some hints today." Cody takes a bite of his bagel, then he leans forward and wipes some whipped cream off my nose with his napkin.

Embarrassed, I take the napkin from him and wipe my face. "Really? Only today? Try again, Detective —"

"I swear, it's the truth."

I look around his small, but tidy home with bookcases brimming with books stacked all the way up to the ceiling. "Funny thing, your house looks pretty normal to me. It doesn't look like a cave or mysterious time traveling-portal. Do you suddenly go to another universe when you cross your threshold?" I tease pointedly.

Cody chuckles. "I only wish it was something that mystical and fun. I like to escape into my books, but that's not what I was doing. Unfortunately, I had family stuff to deal with. I've been across the country dealing with my family in Arizona."

I cringe at his statement. "I wouldn't wish family drama on anyone. I have enough of my own."

"It's okay. You couldn't have known. My parents are better, I think. We knew my grandma would die soon. She's had health issues for years; we just didn't realize my grandpa would follow her so quickly."

"I owe you an apology. I was making all sorts of assumptions based on how people have been treating me lately. That isn't fair to you. You've done nothing wrong. I just find it hard to believe you know nothing about what's happened recently. My name has been dragged through the mud for a solid month."

"I'm sorry. Can you tell me what happened?"

"I don't know. Are you even going to believe me? Nobody else does," I can't help but snap.

"You know, I'm pretty good at sorting out fact and fiction. It's sort of what I do for a living. I'm known for giving people the benefit of the doubt and not pigeonholing people based on stereotypes or my prejudice about a case. I wouldn't be very good at my job if I wasn't," Cody answers defensively.

"I get that. I understand we've been colleagues for a long time … and we have respect for each other. But I've been let down by a lot of people I thought knew me. I mean *really* knew me. All those people seem to have vanished into thin air. I guess these days, I don't know what to expect from you."

"How about you just tell me what happened — rather than assume I'm already guilty of something I haven't done yet?" he challenges.

The quiet confidence in his voice makes me sit up and take notice. Reluctantly, I meet his gaze and concede,

"Touché."

"You know, most of the time you and I are on the same side. I don't expect to change sides anytime soon," he prompts gently.

"Oh you have no idea how quickly things can change. I woke up one morning and everything I thought was true about my life was suddenly false."

"What happened?"

"I don't know. I know I sound like I'm spouting clichés, but it's true. It should have been a high point for me, career-wise. We got that victory against the puppy mill — you know the one providing bait dogs to the dogfighting ring? The DA was shocked the jury came back with punitive damages on the case. He had warned me all along not to pursue charges, but Doctor Stuart Eastwood from The Critter Clinic helped me collect all sorts of genetic information on the dogs I never even knew existed. Mitch from Hope's Haven dug up tons of background on their training methods and we were able to nail them. The defense couldn't argue with a vet with his credentials and a nationally acclaimed trainer of search and rescue dogs. It was a high-profile win for our office."

"Derek Zane should have been thrilled with that outcome," Cody comments as he nurses his coffee.

"Yeah, one would think — especially since I followed it with an even bigger victory."

"That's right. You were the lead prosecutor in the modeling service case, weren't you? My former partner, Dylan, said he had to testify. I guess he did some undercover work on that case."

"Let's be honest. The only modeling involved in the

Boyles case were the selfies those girls took in order to be considered for 'jobs' with that creep," I comment dryly as I make air quotes.

Cody shakes his head and sighs. "You know what they say about karma? The prison system has its own hierarchy. People who take advantage of young girls don't fare very well. He may face his own form of punishment."

"Well, I know better than to comment — because I do believe in karma. I got my victory in court. What happens to him from now on isn't really my concern. I'm just happy he can't victimize any other people."

"You're telling me you were punished because you won two high-profile cases?"

"Not officially, but it sure seems like it. It's weird too — because I was finally feeling worthy of the promotion I got when Fleming passed away."

"What were you officially accused of?"

I set my hot chocolate down on the table and rub my temples. "I swear … I keep expecting this to get easier every time I tell it, but it's still surreal. I can't believe these words are coming out of my mouth. You have to believe me, this isn't even remotely true. I mean, how long have we known each other? I don't know…. what? Nine years? Maybe ten? You have to know this isn't me! I would never do this."

Cody gets up and squats in front of me. He grips my hands. "Do what, Tori?"

I draw in a shaky breath and let it out as a heavy sigh. "I might as well tell you, because like you saw at the gym today everybody assumes I'm guilty and you'll hear sooner or later — probably sooner. I guess I should probably tell you my side. If you're like everyone else, you'll assume the worst anyway."

Cody raises an eyebrow. "Didn't we just have this conversation? I'm usually on your side, remember?"

"Right. We'll see." I let go of Cody's hands, spring to my feet and scoot past him. "I'm sorry, too many years of presenting cases. I'm more comfortable if I can pace while I tell you this. It's how I practice my opening and closing statements."

Cody stands and gestures toward the big picture window. "Be my guest. Do whatever makes you feel comfortable."

"Trust me, none of this will be comfortable," I say as I toe off my shoes and set them by his front door. I walk over to his refrigerator and grab some bottled water, remove the cap, and take a long drink.

As I set the bottle down on the kitchen counter, a shaggy mutt of a dog comes wandering around the corner. "Who is this?" I ask as the dog nuzzles my thigh.

"That's Calico Jack. Every time the refrigerator opens, he thinks he's going to get treats. He's partial to string cheese."

"Aren't you cute?" As I reach down to pet the little spiky-haired terrier, I notice he's missing an eye. "Oh poor baby! What happened to his eye?"

"No one knows. He's one of Dashonte's first rescue dogs after he started working at Stuart's vet clinic. Darya and I were working on a task force together. She has a soft spot for Dashonte. Somehow she convinced me I needed a dog. It turns out she was right. Calico Jack and Darya's two dogs, Atlas and Dozer, go on play dates together all the time."

"You're a good man, Cody Erickson."

"And you're stalling, Tori Clarkson," Cody counters.

"What? He is cute," I protest. I take a deep breath and pause to take a drink of water before I start to pace. "Okay. As near as I can tell, the whole thing started when I was on my way to depose a witness in the puppy mill case. Milton Cavanaugh was the handyman at Eight Paw & Palmdust Kennels. As it turned out, he was much more than that. He handled all the money for the dog fighters, but I didn't know that for sure in the beginning. To me, he was just a witness I needed to depose."

"A real charmer, I'm sure," Cody mutters as he rolls his eyes.

I stop, close my eyes, and lean my head against the wall as I remember the disheveled, perpetually nervous, soft-spoken gentleman. "Actually, he was disarmingly charming in his own way. If you encountered him on the street, you would never guess he was capable of an evil thought. He's one of those men you would guess would have his own little herd of hand-fed pedigreed lapdogs at home. I'll admit I was shocked when I finally figured out how deeply he was involved in the crime ring."

"We all have perps who fool us — but what does he have to do with the demise of your career? Did you let him go or something?"

"Oh, I would be blessed if it was only something so simple —"

"It's funny how that works. Things that blow up in our faces typically aren't so simple."

"That's the weird thing about this. I'll never figure out what role Milton had in this whole nightmare. I don't know if he is the instigator of all my problems or merely an innocent bystander."

"What do you mean?" Cody asks with a puzzled expression.

I yank on my ponytail to tighten the holder. I've given up wearing my hair down because I've developed a nervous tick of twirling my hair so hard it's starting to fall out.

"Let me ask you a question — how much of Anthony's crass conversation did you overhear today?" I ask, bracing myself for the answer.

This time, it's Cody who looks more than a little uncomfortable.

"Probably more than was socially polite for me to overhear. Let's just say I know more about your sexual activities than I should, considering you and I have never dated."

A growl rises from my chest and a stricken expression crosses Cody's face. "Sorry Tori, you asked."

"Remember, those things you heard … they're all rumor and allegations. I didn't actually do those things. I'm not even sure how the rumors got started unless it was from Mr. Cavanaugh's defense team. I barely even touched Mr. Cavanaugh, and I certainly didn't touch him inappropriately," I insist, my voice breaking with emotion.

"I'm sorry if this is difficult to share, but it would help me understand if you could start at the beginning," Cody cajoles.

"You know, that's the odd thing about the story. It doesn't matter how many times I explain it to people, it makes no more sense than it did the first time I tried to piece it together."

"Why don't you give it a shot? I'm great at putting puzzle pieces together."

"We were in the old executive suites where So They Said Court Reporting Services is located. I like to use their offices to take depositions because it's neutral territory. A lot of times, sessions there feel less confrontational than if I ask people to come to the prosecutor's office. I was getting ready to take the elevators up to the conference rooms when the elevator was blocked open by Mr. Cavanaugh and one of the building's cleaning staff. I used the door open button and allowed them to come in."

Cody nods.

"The elevators in that building are old and rickety. They are temperamental at best. On this day, the elevator seemed to pause between floors and Mr. Cavanaugh didn't deal with it well. Honestly, I thought the man might have a heart attack on the spot. He started sweating and silently sobbing. He had a set of rosary beads in his hands. He was audibly praying and running the beads through his fingers. When the elevator settled on our floor, it jerked abruptly. The beads broke and went flying all over the floor."

"Oh no, poor guy."

"At that point, the man dissolved into tears and started openly crying. He started to explain how the beads belonged to his mother. I felt horrible for him. Honestly, at this point, I forgot he was a witness in my case. I just wanted to fix his problem. So, I slipped off my high heels and dropped down to my hands and knees in the tiny little elevator and tried to find several dozen amber colored beads buried in variegated brown carpet in the dark."

"I guess no good deed goes unpunished, huh?"

"You have no idea. I was in the midst of getting the beads off Mr. Cavanaugh's clothes when the elevator opened. Rather than ask me what was happening, his defense attorney made all sorts of assumptions. Four months later, after the trial was complete, and we won, I was hauled in front of my boss and told that if I didn't resign immediately, they would release highly suggestive cell phone footage. They insisted it proved I had been sexually inappropriate with a defense witness and it would completely destroy my career."

"Do you think any evidence exists?"

"Of me being sexually inappropriate? Oh, heck no! It never happened! Of me picking up Mr. Cavanaugh's rosary beads? Maybe. I wasn't paying any attention to what the cleaning staff was doing. He was behind a big utility mop bucket. There was barely room for any of us to move in the tiny elevator. I can imagine he wouldn't have had enough light to film anything — but who knows … with video editing software. The way things were in that elevator, I could've looked like a veritable porn star while I was picking beads off the floor and off of Mr. Cavanaugh. I can't control that, but I do know I wasn't offering anyone any sexual favors at any point. I was there to take a deposition — I just had the stupid luck to try to be nice to someone along the way."

"You're right. The story doesn't make any sense. They simply took one person's word for it and didn't do any investigation. I mean, it's not like the defendant's side would have reason to be biased against the prosecution's office or anything —" Cody's speech trails off.

"I know! Right? It's crazy. People lie about us all the time. For many people, we are the personification of evil.

So why in this one instance did they choose to believe them?"

"I don't know. But I have known you for a long time. You are a fierce competitor. Why didn't you fight back?" Cody asks.

Why didn't I fight back? It's not like I don't ask myself that same question a million times a day.

I lean my head back against the wall and wrap my arms around myself as tears flow down my face.

A voice whispers from my soul.

Why should I have had to?

Chapter Three

Cody

Dylan Palmer doesn't even stop by my desk. He always takes his breaks with me. I crumple up a piece of paper and throw it at his back. "Hey! What's up with you?" He's not even pretending to ration his coffee. Alarmingly, he's carrying the whole pot of pitch-black coffee into his office.

Dylan spins around slowly, his eyes vacant and haunted. He looks like he hasn't slept in weeks. "Tallulah's parents are burying her today."

The hairs on the back of my neck stand up. "What do you mean? I don't remember them saying anything about finding her at the briefing this morning."

Dylan slumps down in the chair next to my desk. "That's just it. We haven't found her. It's like she disappeared off the planet. Her parents just gave up. They can't stand the thought of not knowing. So, they decided to have a funeral to give everyone closure. I know I should be there to support them — they've gone through hell. I should go watch to see if anything looks out of place. But … I just can't."

"I'm so sorry this one hit so close to home. Don't torture yourself. There are other people who work here. You've got options. If I were you, I'd send Pauline. She's spooky good. For a relative rookie, she reads body language better than almost anyone else on our force. Besides, she could pass for one of Tallulah's classmates."

Dylan takes a gulp of coffee. "That's not a bad idea." He sets his cup down next to the coffee pot on my desk. "Be right back!" he says as he runs out of my cubicle.

A few minutes later Dylan returns and sits back down. "I owe you one. I don't think I could've handled coming face-to-face with her family today. Pauline's got my back. Thanks for the suggestion."

"Any time. That's what former partners do," I answer as I hand him a chocolate glazed donut.

He grins at me when he takes it. "I'm already drinking black coffee by the pot so I guess I might as well go all the way with the cliché."

"Nah, it's not about that at all. You're just looking a little shaky. I figure you need some carbs," I tease. "In all seriousness, when was the last time you had a decent night's sleep and a good meal?"

"I am so exhausted, I honestly can't remember. It's been a long time since a case has consumed me like this. When I took the call, I figured it would be a typical runaway case. You know … angsty teenager ticked off at her parents for not letting her see her boyfriend. I figured I'd have her home for a hot pancake breakfast."

"It was a reasonable hunch," I argue.

"Maybe, it seems my hunch was totally wrong. From everything I've been able to determine, Tallulah Johnson simply vanished off the planet. She's a good kid. She has great parents, a run-of-the-mill job for a kid her age and scholarships to go to college next year. She doesn't have boyfriend problems, and everyone seems to like her. She's one of those kids who is beating all the odds. None of the stereotypes seem to apply to her."

"So why is she missing?" I ask rhetorically.

"Beats the heck out of me. I stay up nights trying to figure it out. Don't you have a missing juvenile case too? I thought I heard something —"

"Maybe I have a case. The mom is reluctant to come forward — she doesn't exactly trust the likes of us. Right now, all I've got is a concerned big brother … and a missing sixteen-year-old African-American male."

Dylan leans forward in the chair as he pulls his notebook out of his jacket pocket. "Does he know Tallulah?"

"I get the impression he does. I don't know if they go to school together or live in the same neighborhood. But there is some connection."

"Erickson! What are you waiting for, man? We need to talk to that mom like yesterday!"

"Palmer, she's not even sure she wants the police involved. She's not convinced her son isn't hanging out somewhere playing video games. Dashonte is the one who is concerned about DeAndre."

"So you've been sitting on this?" Dylan asks me in an uncharacteristically critical tone.

"No, I haven't been doing nothing. I've been checking out DeAndre's friends and all his hangouts. Unlike your victim, mine has a history of a few run-ins with law enforcement. I'm checking out his prior accomplices to see if he's fallen off the straight-and-narrow. Dashonte thinks he's still playing it straight, but the family is sometimes the last to know."

"Anything else?"

"Yeah, actually —" I point to a picture on my desk. "Katie's big brother happened to be at the table when Dashonte stopped by to talk. He had a good idea, so I went to talk to Tori Clarkson."

Dylan pulls a sour face. "I'm not sure messing with her will be much help on top of the bad publicity we're getting for not being able to find Tallulah Johnson."

I stop digging through my file folders and whip my head around to look at Dylan. "You knew what was happening with Tori and you didn't say anything?" I demand.

"Well, I figured you were a little busy dealing with actual tragedies. I didn't figure you would want to be bogged down with office gossip and sordid tales of who's sleeping with who."

"I'm surprised at you! I thought you liked Tori. This is a little more than gossiping about the outcome of a reality TV show, Tori lost her job. She's one of the best prosecutors we know."

"I used to think that too, but now there seems to be some open question about her ethics and her methods."

"Only because she hasn't been allowed to tell her side of the story. She's never told anybody what actually happened. People made up stories based on their own agendas. It's too bad the facts didn't actually have anything to do with the truth."

"You know this how?" Dylan presses.

"Because she told me when I asked her. She was

honest about things she wishes she would've done better. I believe her account of what happened."

"Since when do we just take people's word for what they say happened?"

"I can't believe you're being such a jerk about this," I snap. "If that's the way you've got your friends' back, I hope I'm never unjustly accused of anything."

"Think about what you just said for a minute. The best way to help Tori is to find solid evidence to help clear her name and back her story."

"You're right. Except in this case, she's not fighting in front of a jury. She's fighting to win back respect in the court of public opinion."

Dylan slugs back more coffee. "Earning back her reputation could be the hardest fight she's ever faced."

"Let's hope not. The world needs an advocate like Tori."

Mrs. Greeley takes a moment to wipe her face with a Kleenex as she tries to compose herself toward the end of our interview. "I'm sorry I waited so long to talk to you. I guess I was hoping if I ignored the situation, it would go away. DeAndre is my most stubborn child. If I told him bedtime was eight o'clock, I would find him in his room hovered under his blankets with a flashlight playing with his matchbox cars at midnight. He'd look up at me with his big brown eyes and tell me, 'You didn't say I had to be asleep, you said I had to be in bed.' I just figured this was another one of those situations where he was testing the rules, you know what I mean?"

"I understand," I respond with a sympathetic nod. "You've checked in with all of his friends and still nothing?"

"You have no idea! I turned the phone company inside out. I've even checked in with his so-called enemies."

My ears perk up. "Enemies?"

"I dunno if I'd call them enemies so much as ex-friends. It's no secret that my DeAndre hasn't been a perfect angel. When he turned his life around, he had to leave a group of people he thought were his friends behind — you know those punks were not good for him. But I checked — even those people haven't heard from him in months."

"I have one more question. Dashonte mentioned DeAndre might have known Tallulah Johnson. Do you know anything about that?"

Mrs. Greeley smiles wistfully before she chuckles. "Only in his dreams. My little Romeo had a crush on Tallulah — that poor little girl — but she went to a private school. I don't know if he ever got his nerve up to actually talk to her — but he would watch her get on the bus while he waited for his. He'd tell me how pretty she was and how he thought it was cool how she could stand out in a school uniform."

"But as far as you know, they weren't friends or travelled in the same social circle?" I press.

Mrs. Greeley rolls her eyes at me. "Honey, people in my neighborhood clean the houses of people in their neighborhood, so no, probably not." Large tears brim in her eyes and threatened to spill out on her cheeks. She looks at me somberly and asks, "Do you think DeAndre will end up like Tallulah? I heard her poor parents had to bury an empty coffin yesterday. Please don't tell me I'm gonna have to bury my baby?"

"I can't promise anything, Mrs. Greeley — but I'll do everything in my power to stop that from happening."

Chapter Four

Tori

As soon as I place the bags of groceries on the kitchen counter, Bonni Jeanne confronts me. She's holding a piece of paper and she has a thunderous expression on her face. "I'm sorry to leave you in such a lurch, Ms. Clarkson, but I can't do this anymore."

My heart races and my stomach feels like I've swallowed shards of glass. "What did my mom do this time? Whatever it is, I'm sorry. I know she didn't mean to. She can't even rationalize what she does anymore."

"I know, ma'am. But I didn't go to nursing school so I could get spat on all day. I know it's been several years since I've had a nursing license, but I still deserve respect."

"I'm not suggesting you don't, Bonni Jeanne. You've been more than patient with my mom. I'm just begging you for a little more time. I'm taking her to a new specialist next week. It was the earliest I could get in. We've been waiting for this appointment for months. Maybe he'll prescribe a new medication. From what I've been reading, his office participates in all sorts of medical trials. I hope he'll be on the cutting edge of medicine and open to trying some new things with Mom."

"That's what makes this so hard for me. You're trying to be a good daughter. I can see that. I don't want to leave you alone to cope with all this. I understand how hard it is. Like I said, I don't want to leave you in a lurch. But your mother has become nearly impossible. If and I do mean *if* me I stay — I you must find me another respite worker to help me out. I need to go home and discuss this with my own family first though. They're worried about me. This is simply too much responsibility to fall on my shoulders."

My relief is so palpable I want to pass out on the spot. "Thank you, Bonni Jeanne. I'll work on finding someone to help you tomorrow."

"I don't want to sound greedy, but you might want to think about paying us a little more too. Your mom is getting worse by the day and she's more than a handful. If I can be candid, you really ought to consider putting your mom in a facility which specializes in memory issues. I don't know how much longer it'll be safe to keep her at home."

I sink down onto a barstool at the breakfast bar. "I've always known this day would come sooner or later. I promised my daddy I wouldn't do that to her. We were supposed to stay a family."

Bonni Jeanne clicks her tongue at me as she shakes her head in dismay. "Now, I can't rightly say I knew your Papa, but if you're anything to judge him by, I bet he was an honorable man. I bet he wouldn't want you to destroy yourself to save your mama, right? If he knew how bad things were, I'm sure he wouldn't want you to put yourself in danger to take care of your mom. That's what things are coming down to, you know. That's why you need to consider putting her in a safer environment. I watch her carefully, but sometimes I can't catch everything."

I nod. "Oh, I know that all too well."

"The other day I was making her tea at her request and I turned around to fill the teapot with water. By the time I turned back, your mom had a box of matches and was trying to light the electric burners on the stove. As if the matches weren't bad enough, your mother had all four burners turned to high heat while she was trying to light the matches. I only had my back turned for two-seconds while I was filling the teapot at the sink. I'm sorry if my admission means you think less of my care taking skills, I'm just trying to be honest with you about the danger your mother is in."

"No, I totally understand. The other day, I had to take an important phone call. While I was on the phone, she managed to get over to the neighbor's house. She tried to convince the neighbors' grandchildren she was their grandmother. I don't have any kids. The neighbors were understandably creeped out. Fortunately, they know my mom has dementia, and they didn't call the police, although they had every right to."

"We've both been lucky. Things could have been much worse. I hate to tell you this because I love your mother like family. If the new medicine doesn't change things, you need to make some changes — for your mom's health and for your own sanity."

"Thank you for the reality check. I just need all this to hold together for a little while longer. My life is complete chaos right now and I can't fix everything all at once," I admit. My voice breaks as a tear rolls down my cheek.

"Don't cry," Bonni Jeanne admonishes, as she awkwardly pats my back. "Today was an incredibly trying day. I'll be back tomorrow and the next day. Maybe you're right and a doctor somewhere will be able to get the spider webs out of your mom's brain and it will work the way it used to. I can't help but think if your mother understood what was going on around her, she would be the most dismayed of everyone."

"I know she would. My mom used to be so proud of all the things she knew off the top of her head. She could recite the presidents and the vice presidents and the state capitals. Most school kids know how to do similar feats. However, most people don't commit the school each one graduated from to memory. My mom rarely used a cookbook. Once she saw a recipe in a magazine or newspaper, she knew exactly what it called for and how to make it. Dementia has been an especially cruel joke to play on a woman like her."

"It's so hard to watch people become a shadow of their former selves. The only blessing, I think, is I doubt your mom has any awareness of the things she used to be able to do. All this is toughest on those of us who have to watch from the sidelines and try to make it all better."

I reach out and embrace Bonni Jeanne. "I'm so lucky to have you in my life. Thank you for taking such great care of my mom. I know I don't always stop and take the time to tell you how much that means to me — especially now with everything that's going on — but you're a lifesaver. Thank you."

"You're welcome Ms. Clarkson … uh … Tori, I didn't mean to sound ungrateful or hateful toward your mother. I love her like my own kin. But sometimes, she's just too much to handle."

"I'm already persuaded Bonni Jeanne. I'll work on changing things tomorrow. Thanks for sticking by me."

"It's okay. We're a team."

Just as Bonni Jeanne makes her consolatory comments, my mom lets out a bloodcurdling scream from her bedroom. From the sound of the chanting coming from the room, it sounds as if her mind is stuck somewhere in her childhood as she frantically searches for her doll.

Bonni Jeanne cringes. "It might take both of us to get her settled down from this one. She seems especially far away from reality today."

CHAPTER FIVE

CODY

I KNOCK ON DYLAN'S door and peek my head inside. He sticks his finger up in the air as he says goodbye to the person he's speaking with on the phone. He waves me in, and I sit down.

"You look better today," I observe.

"Yeah, it's amazing what a couple days off will do. What's up?"

"I just got a text from Darya. They've got a missing fifteen-year-old girl in her county. At first, they thought it was a parental abduction, but they put the dad and stepmom on a polygraph and interviewed their employers. It appears they had nothing to do with it."

Dylan swears under his breath. "Why don't we have some freaking task force going on this? This is like the fourth kid in six months!"

I walk over to the table in Dylan's office and slap my file down on the table. "I don't know what to tell you. I can't even convince anybody DeAndre is missing. They all think he's a bad kid. My problem is I have nothing other than my gut to prove them wrong. Everything in the file says he's trouble and going to be one of those kids in and out of the system his whole life. But everyone I've interviewed — clear down to the janitor at the school — says they've seen a real change in him. He was interested in becoming a soldier like his brother or even a police officer like us. It's like he did a whole one-eighty with his attitude."

Dylan shakes his head in dismay. "Right? I mean we preach and preach that we need to catch these kids early and turn them around. But then, by some miracle, when they do, we don't give them any credit for it."

"Mrs. Greeley has worked miracles with those kids. She is a tough warrior. She's sick and fights her own battles with high blood pressure and liver problems but her boys are fine young men. I talked to DeAndre a few times when I was helping to investigate the case of the animal torturers we had a few years ago. Even then, although he was trying really hard to be a bad news punk, I had a feeling about him. He seemed to have an intrinsic goodness and integrity about him even though he was trying to fit in with the rougher kids in his neighborhood. I never bought his story that he was one of the bad guys."

Dylan walks over and starts to leaf through a file. He pauses for a moment and studies the picture of DeAndre. It's one of those quintessential school pictures. DeAndre looks like he's all arms and braces. He is the antithesis of cool. He just looks hopelessly young.

"Do you suppose that could be the reason he has disappeared? Gang activity isn't as bad as it was a few years ago when the white supremacy group was pitting the gangs against each other, but it's still pretty bad. If one of them thought DeAndre was working with law enforcement, it could've been a retaliation thing."

"I suppose it could've been. None of the witnesses I've spoken to have mentioned it — but you know how it goes. I hear a fraction of what actually happens in the neighborhood."

"What does his brother say? As I recall, he was pretty tuned into tensions in the neighborhood. Wasn't he a CI for us at one point?"

"Informally, I suppose. Dashonte hasn't reported an uptick in gang activity. Then again, he's busy studying to be a veterinarian in college. So, he hasn't been as plugged in as he was when he was in high school. He may not be aware of what his little brother is facing."

"It's great for him. I know Stuart says Dashonte is awesome with the dogs. Still, I hate to lose our source on the streets. We need as much information in these cases as we can get."

"I think the reason we can't get any traction on this case in the media besides the demographics of the victim is because in every case there seems to be another logical explanation why the kids could be missing. That's enough to give the media the cover it needs to justify moving on to more glamorous stories."

"Bull!" Dylan insists as he slams his coffee cup down on the table. "There isn't one logical reason on the planet Tallulah Johnson should be gone. She was a great kid with awesome grades and a bright future. She fought with no one. She was responsible, she had a job and she never even got a traffic ticket. By all accounts, she had the kind of relationship with her boyfriend they write poems and songs about. I've been digging for months and I haven't found a single credible reason why Tallulah Johnson shouldn't simply walk in the front door of her house and give her parents a hug."

I sigh. "You're right. Let me amend my statement. Some of the victims present other reasons why they might be missing and that gives people some sort of permission to excuse their disappearance as if somehow they deserved it. That's just wrong. I don't understand why the local and national news isn't leading with these stories every day until these kids are found."

"You know what the news media likes? They like an update to an old story. Would these disappearances tie into an older story? What if they have something to do with the animal torture case? I mean after all, we found that kid in the back of the truck the day Darya was attacked. Who's to say these kids weren't abducted in a situation like that?"

"Or what if it's like John Ashford theorizes?" I add. "He thinks it sounds a lot like the bust Ketki helped with. What if it's like that creepy couple, the Brennans', who are targeting runaways?"

"One problem with your theory; we haven't established that any of the kids are actually runaways."

"I wasn't directly involved with the Brennan case, but if I recall, I don't think all of those kids were willing runaways either. I think Tori worked on the case. The original prosecutor went back to England, so I can't exactly reach out to her. Tori was second chair. She probably remembers."

Dylan raises an eyebrow. "You know she's not working these days, right?"

"I know — but I also know Tori. If there are kids involved, she'll move heaven and earth to help. It can't hurt to ask her."

"I'm no expert, but I think it's a terrible strategy. It's

like rubbing salt in her wounds. Asking her to do a job she's not allowed to do right now seems unspeakably cruel."

I grab my file off the table. "I wish I could argue with you, but I can't. You're right. But I'm out of other options. I've beat the bushes and I have no other ideas. Mrs. Greeley calls me every morning and every night to see if I have any news. Dashonte comes in the office every other day. I have to find answers. I just hope Tori understands why I have to be a jerk."

"You mean, more than your baseline level of jerk — ?" Dylan teases.

"Oh shut up! I don't see you volunteering to take one for the team. I hope you realize I may be sacrificing my future dating relationship with Ms. Clarkson for the sake of finding some missing kids."

Dylan clears his throat. "Yeah, right! If you and Tori had a shot at a future together, you guys would've sorted that out a long time ago. Go solve your case — just be gentle."

"For the record, I don't try to be a jerk."

"Uh-huh … I've been on stake outs with you and heard your voicemails. You're as single as I am. If you and I were ideal partners, we'd be married like Katie and Darya. I've concluded it's all on us."

I heave a heavy sigh. "You might have a point— but I can't figure it out right now. I have to go find missing puzzle pieces so I can solve this case and find some kids."

"Good luck — with everything. I mean it."

Spinning the rope, I jump a few times and attempt to appear casual while I wait for Tori to appear for her regular workout.

When Tori comes to the door, she has her phone to her ear. She looks distraught. I throw down the jump rope and rush toward her. She sees the trainer across the room and looks up with tears in her eyes. "I'm sorry, Suzanne; I can't come to class tonight. I have to go to the hospital."

"That's all right, Tori. Don't worry about it. Do you want me to call you a ride?"

Tori spins around on her foot. She sways and nearly falls. I help steady her. "Don't worry about it. I've got Tori. I can get her to the hospital more quickly than Uber."

"Okay, but what about my car?" she asks.

"I can take care of that later. Where are we going?"

Tori looks at me blankly for a moment. "Umm … Bonni Jeanne said they took Mom to North Florida Regional Medical."

I grab my duffel bag and throw it over my shoulder as I open the door for Tori. I help her into my Mustang and buckle her belt. As I get on the freeway to go toward North Florida Regional, I try to make small talk. "I just realized I know nothing about your family. Is your mom sick?"

Tori nods as she wipes away tears. "Yes, my mother is very sick — but not in the way you might imagine."

"Oh, I see. Depression is common among the

elderly. When I was a beat cop, I was always surprised how many calls I went on that were related to anxiety or depression among seniors."

"You have no idea how I wish it was something as treatable as that." Tori says, as she wraps her arms around herself.

"Oh, I'm so sorry. I just assumed."

"My mom has dementia. I started noticing little things about six years ago. She couldn't remember her friends' names or how to make recipes she's made for years. She struggled to find familiar ingredients in the refrigerator and the pantry even though they were in the same place they'd always been for years. It was heartbreaking when she started to struggle for words. These days, she barely talks anymore. When she does, she often sounds like a child — a very lost, confused child."

"I'm so sorry to hear that. Is Bonni Jeanne your sister?"

Tori lets out a startled laugh. "Bonni Jeanne is my angel. She provides respite care service for me. She takes care of my mom when I can't. Tonight, I guess my mom heard me leave. She tried to follow me and fell down my front stairs. According to Bonni Jeanne, Mom thought I'd be late for school and she needed to drive me. Did I mention she had just gotten out of the tub and was stark naked?"

"Wow! How did that happen? Isn't your care provider supposed to be watching her?"

"Bonni Jeanne is afraid I'm going to fire her for letting Mom get away from her — but, I understand. My mom can look docile and seem timid and frail one moment. The next moment, she has the strength of ten men and can run like Usain Bolt. It's not really Bonni Jeanne's fault. I've had a few close calls myself."

"Is there anything I can do to help?" I ask.

"I have no idea. I don't even know what this means for my mom. We were barely hanging on before, and Mom probably broke her hip. Now, one more thing in my life is up in the air. I have no clue how I'll manage it all. My daddy has been gone a long time, but I sure do miss his strength in times like this."

I reach across the car and grasp her hand. "Tori, I hope you know this. I'm here for you if you need me. All you have to do is ask."

"I appreciate that, Cody. I do. It's just that at this point, I don't even know what I need."

"I understand — but when you do know, don't forget I'm here."

Tori looks up at me through her tears. "I don't think there's any danger of that. You seem to keep showing up in my life at all the wrong times."

Chapter Six

Tori

I CAN BARELY KEEP my eyes open when Cody comes into the room carrying coffee and an overnight bag for me. I can't contain my surprise as I blurt, "What are you doing back here? I thought you went home."

"I did — or, more precisely, I took Bonni Jeanne home after we retrieved your car from the gym. She is a treasure. She kept telling me I look just like her son. I thought she was just being polite, but then she invited me inside and showed me a picture. It was like looking in a mirror. Jean Franco is a firefighter. I'm surprised we haven't crossed paths before. It would be a little disconcerting to run into him on the job."

"That was very nice of you, but it doesn't explain why you didn't just go home. Don't you have to work tomorrow?"

"I do — but you need some company. It wouldn't be the first time I've pulled an all-nighter. I'm a seasoned police detective. I've been on more than a few stakeouts in my career. I'm sure this will be less intense. Besides, I brought goodies," I whisper.

"I'm surprised they let you up here. You're not family or anything."

I shrug. "Maybe I just look like I belong. How is your mom?"

"She has a non-displaced fracture in her hip. She doesn't understand she needs to stay still, so they've sedated her to keep her from injuring herself. I have to remind myself she's not as sick as she looks right now. They're doing this to protect her. She is just a little dehydrated, so they're replenishing her fluids before she has to have orthopedic surgery tomorrow."

"You look wiped out. Do you want to go grab a bite to eat?" Cody offers.

I glance back at my mom. Even on a good day, my mom barely acknowledges my existence … and today is decidedly not a good day. I doubt she even knows I'm in the room.

Cody is patiently waiting for me to weigh my options. Finally, he adds, "We can leave our cell phone numbers and they can text us if there are any developments."

I stand up and stretch. "Yeah, how silly of me. For someone who spends as much time on my cell phone as I do, you'd think I'd never forget other people can still reach out to let me know what's going on." Impulsively, I throw my arms around his neck and give him a hug. "Thank you. Until this very moment, I didn't realize how much I need to take just a few moments to clear my head."

Cody pulls me close and holds me for a few moments. The warmth of his embrace is exactly what I need. I snuggle closer and he brushes a light kiss across my temple as he murmurs, "Whatever you need. I'm your guy."

I pull out of his arms and grab my purse. "Thanks. Right now, I need to get out of here and stop thinking about all the things which could've gone wrong."

Cody puts his hand at the small of my back and escorts me out of the room. We walk around the hospital grounds and we end up in a little garden area, Cody turns to me and asks, "Do you mind if we talk about something completely different for a moment?"

"That might be a welcome distraction. All I can think about right now is how my world is going to change. I don't know how to make all the right choices for my mom. It's hard because she can't even lucidly express what she wants or talk with me about the decisions I need to make."

"Do you have any family I need to call?" Cody offers.

"No, I wish I did. It's just me. My dad had a heart attack when I was still in elementary school. I'm an only child. It's just been me and my mom for many years. It all falls on my shoulders."

"I wish there was something I could do to help you," Cody says as his thumb rubs a particularly tender spot between my shoulder blades were all the tension has settled.

I moan. "Well, you could follow me around all day and give me a back rub."

"If I didn't have to take down bad guys for a living, that would be an exceedingly tempting offer. How about if we grab sandwiches and dessert at the deli instead?"

"Sounds good. Can we not talk about the overwhelming amount of choices I have to make when it comes to my mom? I just want twenty minutes of free time where we can talk about anything else. Your job, baseball scores, weird videos on YouTube, it doesn't really matter to me. I need to stop thinking about my mom, dementia and how much pain she's in."

"I'm not sure talking about my job is going to relieve much of your stress. We have a bunch of missing teenagers. Actually, that's why I was at the gym today. I was hoping to talk to you about some of your cases to see if they overlap with the missing children. Maybe there is a pattern you can recognize from a case you've handled."

I want to burst out crying, but I think I used all the tears available in my body earlier when I saw my mom in so much pain laying on the gurney. "As much as I would love to help you find whoever is lost, I can't. I can't help you or anyone else. It should be abundantly clear to you by now that I can't even help myself."

"I don't need you to have an official title or anything. We can work on fixing your employment mess later. Right now I just need your expertise. I'm out of ideas and I need a fresh perspective. You are one of the smartest people I know."

"Yeah, so smart I got pushed out of my job when I did nothing wrong. That just smacks of brilliance right there, doesn't it?" I retort bitterly.

Cody gathers me into a hug again. He tenderly kisses me on the forehead. As cliché as it sounds, I want to melt into his arms. I could so get used to the feeling of being sheltered from life.

"You can't blame yourself for the stupidity of others," he admonishes softly.

"I know. But sometimes the unfairness of it all seems

overwhelming. I suppose it might help if I look at the problems of someone else for a change. How can I help you?" I offer as I move out of his arms and sit down in a quiet corner of the deserted dining area beside the small deli.

Cody sits down beside me and pulls out a weathered police notebook and pen. "I've got at least three teenagers, and most likely four, who seemingly have nothing in common. Some kids are classified as at risk, but others seemingly have no risk factors at all."

In a heartbeat, the analytical part of my brain clicks on as if nothing is amiss in my life. "Race?"

"One African-American teenage male, age sixteen, one African-American female also age sixteen, one Hispanic fifteen-year-old female, and one Caucasian male, age fifteen."

I flinch at his matter-of-fact recitation of the names. "No connection through their school, church, or social media?"

"Not as far as we can tell. I know two of the victims are from the same neighborhood, but there is no evidence they actually knew each other. They went to two different schools. These are disappearances over the last six months. They seem unrelated — and they very well may be — but something in my gut tells me they're not."

"Do you have anything other than your gut feeling?"

"Well, you remember my former partner, Katelyn Ashford?"

"The one who was shot on the job?"

I nod. "Her brother, John is tied into Savannah Moore's family. He thinks this sounds a lot like that case. He wanted me to ask you if you thought it could possibly be those perps."

A chill passes up my spine. "If it is related to those two, you've got a huge problem on your hands. The Brennans are the personification of evil if you ask me. We know for sure it's probably not them personally, because their sentences are so long, the two of them will never see the light of day. We charged all the co-conspirators we could find, but that doesn't mean we got them all."

"Could they still be running things behind the scenes?"

"I suppose so. It's not unheard of — remember Warren Jepps? He ran his whole enterprise from prison. It barely seemed to slow him down."

"This would seem to be a change in MO for them though. Didn't they target kids who were actually runaways and didn't have a support system?"

"The Brennan's ability to adapt their forms of terror to whatever situation they were in made them uniquely savage predators, in my mind. They used a completely different form of grooming and lures for Savannah than they were using on victims like Ketki, had she not been involved in the police sting."

"I forgot about that aspect of it. You're right, who's to say they haven't adapted their strategy again since they were caught," Cody comments as he takes more notes.

"I don't want you to jump to too many conclusions; I don't even have the files in front of me. I have no idea whether the Brennans have access to any computers while they are incarcerated. If I remember correctly, they were not supposed to be in contact with each other. Their attorney was going to appeal, so I don't know if the provision of the sentence stood up on appeal. I certainly don't know if they're working with people on the outside. It was just a thought."

"Tori, we've all been working on this case since the first child disappeared almost six months ago. I wasn't expecting you to solve it over dinner. I'm just looking for threads to pull together to make sense of it all. Who knows, I could be chasing down more dead ends. All of these cases could indeed be unrelated. Still, I have to do something. I can't stand by and watch more kids disappear under my nose."

"I get it. I just feel terrible because my hands are tied. I want to help you, but I have no access to any of my files. If I ask other people to help, it jeopardizes their jobs. I can't do that to them."

"I'm not asking you to. What you gave me tonight is a place to start. I wish I could return the favor."

"So do I. It'd be nice to know why I lost my job. It has to be something more than just professional jealousy, racism, or sexism. I've faced all that stuff before and still succeeded. This is something bigger."

"You can't quit fighting. You were a natural fit for Assistant District Attorney. You're one of the best prosecutors I've ever seen. Stand up and advocate for yourself. It's what you do best. Now, you need to make yourself your client."

Shooting to my feet, I walk over and poke him in the chest. "It must be nice to make decisions for me. But you have no idea what I've been coping with for the past three years. My job is only a small portion of the hell that I'm dealing with right now. In case you forgot, I'm trying to keep my mother alive. It's harder than you think when the woman who used to love you doesn't always remember she even knows you. Speaking of that, I need to get back to her room. So, any further lectures on how I should be living my life will need to wait."

I spin on the ball of my foot and storm off toward my mother's room. I resolve not to look back. Maybe Cody and I are just not meant to be. I've got too much other stuff to worry about right now. I don't need someone telling me how I need to save the world. I can barely save myself.

Beep … Beep … Beep … Beep! I sit straight up looking frantically around for whatever monitor alarm is sounding. To my amazement, I'm not in the hospital. This is my bedroom, and that's my alarm clock! *How in the heck did I get here?* I scramble out of bed and yank my alarm clock out of the wall as I struggle to turn it off.

I glance down at myself and realize I'm still wearing the same workout clothes I wore to my exercise class before Bonni Jeanne called me to tell me that my mom had fallen yesterday.

I bolt to the bathroom and take care of business. Vaguely, I wonder how long I've been asleep. I'm shocked when I look in the mirror and see my bloodshot eyes. Wearily, I brush my teeth and throw my hair up in a ponytail. I quickly return to my room and choose clean clothes and try to puzzle through the sequence of events which brought me back to my house.

Suddenly, I hear a noise outside my bedroom door.

Instinctively, I grab a heavy lamp and stand next to

the door as it slowly opens. My heart is racing as I hear a familiar voice ask, "Hey Tori, are you ready for breakfast?"

I exhale heavily as I clutch the lamp to my chest. "Darn it, Cody! You scared me half to death. What are you doing here? Better yet, what am *I* doing here?"

Cody's eyes widen when he sees my improvised weapon.

"You're not gonna clobber me with that when I answer you, are you?"

I raise an eyebrow. "I suppose it depends on your answer."

"Can I set this down?" Cody asks as he nods toward the tray of food he's carrying.

"Where'd you get all that food?" I demand.

Cody shrugs. "I made it."

"Out of the stuff in my kitchen?" I ask incredulously.

"It was a bit of a challenge. But with a little creativity, it came together."

Not knowing what else to do, I set the lamp down and walk back over to my bed and crawl under the covers.

"Oh great, now I get to serve you breakfast in bed. It won't quite be a surprise, but it'll still be nice."

"Cody Dewayne Erickson! You still haven't answered my question. Why am I here and not at the hospital with my mom?"

"How did you know my middle name?" Cody deflects.

"Cody!" I warn as my frustration grows. "Answer my question. I know your middle name because I've deposed you before, did you forget?"

Cody salutes me before he picks up the tray and crawls into bed with me.

"No ma'am, I did not forget your phenomenal skills as an attorney. You're here because you needed help. Apparently, the emotion of the night caught up with you and you passed out from the sheer emotion or exhaustion of the moment."

"Oh my gosh! How embarrassing. I don't even remember."

"It's okay; I don't think the nurses will hold it against you."

I look around my room frantically trying to figure out what time it is. I mentally curse myself when I remember I screwed up my alarm clock when I was turning it off. "I need to get back to the hospital. My mom is by herself," I blurt in a panicked voice. "My mom has been all alone in the hospital for hours!" I sob. "How could I be so irresponsible?"

Cody puts his arm around me and holds me as deep sobs wrack my body. "Shh, Tori, listen to me. Your mom isn't there by herself. Bonni Jeanne is there and Crystal Downing went to keep her company. Your mom is fine. I've been checking in every two hours. She's resting comfortably."

I sag against Cody in relief. "Oh, they didn't have to do that."

"I know. But they wanted to because they care about you. Why don't you eat some breakfast? It's going to be a long day. Your mom has to have surgery today."

"Oh gosh, they were supposed to do that the first thing this morning. We'll be late!" I exclaim as I try to leave the bed.

"Tori, stop. You need to eat. We have plenty of time before the surgery. You work out insanely early in the morning, remember?"

"No! You stop!" I snap as I pull away from him. I grab some clothes and head toward the bathroom calling back over my shoulder, "You don't have the right to tell me what to do. You don't know what this is like. My mom counts on me to be there. I'm the only person she has — even if she doesn't know that."

Right before I turn the shower on I hear Cody say in a resigned voice, "I wasn't trying to offend you, I was just trying to help you take care of yourself so you can take care of your mom."

I lean my head up against the cold tile in the shower and let the freezing water flow over me. I'm too frustrated with myself to let it warm up. I suppose that's my punishment for being an ungrateful witch.

The logical side of me knows Cody is a good guy who's trying his best to help out in a difficult situation, but the side of me who's in the middle of a meltdown can't get over the injustice of it all.

Chapter Seven

Cody

DYLAN CATCHES ME AS I'm headed to the supply room to get another stack of notebooks. He taps me on the shoulder and I nearly drop everything I'm carrying. "Are you ever going to go home, or should the captain start charging you rent?"

I shrug. "I've got things to do, people to meet, cases to solve … you know the drill."

"I do know the drill — but I also know you're doing everything yourself. Some of these cases haven't even been assigned to you. You could have the officers in charge actually handle their own cases."

"I know, but I'm chasing down a lead Tori gave me the other day. It's important that I ask the same questions the same way to everyone to make sure I get consistent answers."

Dylan runs his hand through his hair. "Look, I'm not gonna question the way you do your job. But you need to watch yourself. You don't want to get burned out. I know you want to find these kids, but you can't kill yourself in the process."

I chuckle. "That's funny coming from you. I swear you and I just had this conversation a few weeks ago."

"We did. That's why I recognize all the symptoms. You need to go home and get some rest, so you can find some objectivity."

"Okay, fine. I was about to wrap it up here anyway. I'm planning to take a three-day weekend."

"Now you're talking! Go take Tori on a date or something productive. You know, like normal people do?"

"I'd love to, but I don't think she's talking to me."

"What in the heck did you do to her this time?"

"I stepped in it. I stuck my nose where it shouldn't have been and I gave my opinion about things I knew nothing about. I got a little taste of Tori Clarkson's famous fiery temper. I suppose I deserved it too, but that doesn't make it suck any less."

"So that's it? You're just gonna give up because the lady got mad at you?"

"Nah, not my plan. I'm simply regrouping. I've decided to put my money where my mouth is. I try not to be repeatedly stupid if I can help it."

"Well, I hope you decide to do all this after you take a shower and a nap. At this very moment, you are the definition of disgusting . I hope you are awake enough to have that degree of self- awareness," Dylan teases.

"I do. I have spent a crazy amount of time today trying to decide whether the first thing I'll do when I get home is shower and take all the grime off or collapse into bed for twenty-four hours straight."

"That's a tough call. When I'm in your shoes, I always

tried to decide whether I can stay awake long enough to take a shower without drowning. If the answer is no, I sleep first."

"Good call. Sleep it is." I answer as I sling my backpack over my shoulder. "See you in a few days."

"Don't do anything I wouldn't do," Dylan teases.

"You've been telling me that same lame joke for years. You know I never pay attention."

"Well, maybe one day you will."

"Probably not today," I call over my shoulder. It's a good thing Dylan doesn't know how true that statement is.

Crystal looks around Art Your Heart Out with wide eyes. "This is such a cool place. I can't believe I've never been here." She chuckles softly to herself. "Then again, I can believe it. I'm not very crafty."

"You didn't want anyone to know you were meeting with me, so I chose a spot where you were unlikely to ever go so you wouldn't run into your friends."

Crystal laughs out loud. "That's true, they'd never think to look for me here."

Nancy, the owner, who's been walking several steps behind us, suddenly speeds up and opens the door. "This is a room I've always intended to make into a classroom. At the moment, it's just an overflow room." She hands me a set of keys. "Make yourself comfortable. There's water in the refrigerator. Cody, when you're done, you can lock up my shop and take the keys over to Ink'd Deep.

Jade is working on a new tattoo for me. I'll be there for several hours."

"Thank you, Nancy. I appreciate your help."

"Don't mention it. I can never thank you enough for all you did for my family. My daughter and my granddaughter are happy and healthy in no small part because of what you and your colleagues have done. If I can help you keep other people safe, it's the least I can do."

Nancy waves at Crystal and gives her a thumb's up as she turns and walks out of her store.

Nervously, Crystal walks over and sits down on the couch. I pull up a rolling office chair and sit down across from her.

"Thank you so much for coming to talk to me today. I want you to know I'm not here in an official capacity. I'm here as Tori's friend."

"Okay, that's nice. But why isn't anything being officially done?"

"I don't know the answer to that quite yet. Hopefully, what I find will help me come up with answers about why nothing seems normal in Tori's case."

"So, nothing I say to you will be public, right?"

"Right now, this isn't even an official investigation. I'm not filing any reports or making any statements. Right now we're just having a conversation between friends. It's off the record until you want to make a statement on the record."

Crystal wilts back against the couch. "Oh good, I'm so glad someone else thinks everything that's happening is weird. I've worked for a lot of prosecutors in my years.

You know, I'm almost old enough to retire — don't tell anybody. I always lie to my friends about my age. Nobody really knows how old I am. Let me just tell you this — some of the people here are the kids of the people I started with. But I've never, ever seen anything like what happened to Tori."

"Can you explain what you saw?"

"I don't know if I can explain it. It was just too strange. Almost everybody likes Tori, but some folks never will. I'll just put that out there. Some people are jealous because she's really, really good at her job. Some people are mad because she's a woman and they don't think women should be in powerful positions. I know that's true. It shouldn't be, but it is. It was true when I started and it's still true now."

"Sadly, we see some of that in the police department as well."

"There are even a few people who don't think Tori earned her new position honestly because she's black. They think somehow she cheated. I know that's not true because I know how hard she works. She works rings around the other attorneys in our office. Even though her mama is sick, she works longer hours and tougher cases. The paralegals tell me she even adds cases to their briefs, and she'll spend hours crafting her arguments and studying juries."

"I know that kind of discrimination exists too. It doesn't matter how hard you work or what you've accomplished, someone will always assume you got your job because of your race — not in spite of it. It's always been a problem, but it's far worse now. As politics grows uglier, so does systemic discrimination."

"All that's true — the sexism and the racism, but this seemed more than that —"

"That's weird. Tori said the same thing," I interrupt.

"I'm not surprised she picked up on it. There's like a weird undercurrent. Even though she hasn't been in the office for a while, I'm sure people have been gossiping so loud she must be able to hear in the community. We have some sort of gag order, but I can't bear to stay quiet and let Tori suffer by herself."

"When did the undercurrents start?"

"To be honest, there have been a few waves of weird undercurrents. The first wave started a few years ago when Derek Zane came on board. Everything about Mr. Zane is flashy. It's big, bold and exaggerated. Some people like that kind of stuff and a lot of the attorneys in the office were falling all over themselves to impress him and, frankly, date him. He considers himself quite a catch. I suppose I see the appeal. He looks kinda like a movie star — if you catch him in the right light. Anyway, he has a high opinion of himself and he doesn't mind sharing it."

"What did Tori think of Mr. Zane?"

"Officially? They had no problems. Publicly, she tried to be supportive of whatever he did. Privately, she thought he should spend a lot less time grooming his public persona and his hair and dedicate a lot more time to learning the cases his office was handling and going after the true bad guys."

"I take it Tori didn't have a high opinion of how Derek was handling the position of district attorney?"

"Oh, I think it was more than that," Crystal answers with a wry chuckle. "She found him downright repulsive."

"Tori isn't one to mince words. That must've been interesting."

"She actually did a pretty good job of keeping her opinions to herself. However, Derek Zane had his eye on Tori. He wanted her to be one of his office conquests. It drove him crazy that she didn't want to go out with him. I don't have to tell you that Tori is beautiful. Mr. Zane made it a point to go out with all the most gorgeous women. He likes to go to all the high-profile events with beautiful arm candy. If the arm candy was smart, all the better. So, when Tori rebuffed his advances, even as polite as she was, that didn't go over well."

"What do you mean? Can you give me some examples?"

Crystal's expression tightens. "It was just stupid little unprofessional stuff that shouldn't be happening in an office. You know, it got awful around the holidays when we have all the parties and get-togethers. Whenever Tori would show up alone to one of those, Derek would make some sort of remark like, 'Well, it's no surprise the Ice Princess is alone. No one in their right mind would put up with someone like her.' It was demoralizing for Tori."

"I can imagine."

"For a while, a bunch of random stuff started going wrong with her car. Her tires would go flat, her gas cap would mysteriously go missing, and her gas was suddenly siphoned off. When she tried to report it to security, Mr. Zane told her that if she had a good man in her life, that kind of stuff wouldn't happen to her."

"What a load of garbage!" I exclaim. "Please tell me she reported this crap?"

"Reported what to who exactly? Tori couldn't prove that Derek had done anything wrong. He could say he just has an offbeat sense of humor. He didn't make any overt threats at that point, he hadn't even penalized her — he just specialized in making her feel inferior and stupid."

"What a jerk!"

"Yeah, that's not even half of it. He loved to take credit for everyone else's work. That's just idiotic in an office like ours. We build cases as a team — but make no mistake; we know who doesn't pull their weight. We also know who busts their butt to pull out a win, even when the odds are against us. Tori is that kind of prosecutor. She should not have lost her job."

"I agree with you one hundred percent. You said the undercurrents occurred in waves, what happened next?"

"After a while, people started ignoring the digs from Derek and he moved on. I thought things would calm down. They did for a while — but then Mr. Fleming had a heart attack and Tori was promoted into his position. It was the right thing to do. She was next in line. Most folks here had no problem with that. It was her job fair and square."

"Of course. Tori wouldn't want it any other way."

"Then shortly after the elections, people from Councilman Warren's office came sniffing around. They started interviewing all of us — real subtle like — it was very odd. They wanted to know how happy we were with Tori. They asked very strange questions. 'Did she do a good job? Did we like working with her? Was she working in the interests of the county? Was she honest and trustworthy? Had she ever done anything to make us feel uncomfortable?' They said it was all confidential. They made it sound like she was up for some sort of special honor. At the time, it made sense because she had just had victories in those two high-profile cases and just been promoted. Most of our staff likes Tori, and they were happy she got hired as the assistant district attorney when Mr. Fleming died, so they cooperated with the questioning because they thought they were doing her a favor."

"Of course, they did. Because what else would it be, right?" I comment as I pause and turn the page on my notebook.

"See? Now me, I had my thinking cap on. I didn't believe them for a New York minute. Something was fishy from the get-go. Like I said, I've been around for a long time. I've seen people get big honors. I once worked for somebody who got an honor from President Bush — the junior one. They didn't ask those kinds of questions. It seemed like a real big set-up for a big fall. I didn't want to answer the questions. My boss told me I had to — otherwise I'd be written up. So, I answered their stupid questions. I kept my answers super general. Of course, I made Tori look like the best thing since sliced bread because you know she is. The only negative thing I said was she made me feel uncomfortable one year because she forgot my birthday. It was a true statement. But it wasn't her fault — she had the flu."

"Do you know what became of the questioning?" I ask.

Crystal gives me a look that would wither grown trees. "We have a new prosecutor in our office."

"Oh… I wasn't aware that they had filled Tori's position," I blurt as I cough in surprise.

"Umm-hmm, Stacy Hildabrand started a couple weeks ago." Crystal looks like she's been sucking on lemons.

"Care to comment on that development?"

"Not really. I've got grand-babies to raise and I need my job. Let's just say, I took the extra step to call her law school to confirm that she actually graduated and that her diploma isn't fraudulent."

"Okay… Enough said."

"Apparently, she actually passed the bar too. Although for the life of me, I can't imagine how."

"I know I probably don't even have to ask you this, but just for the sake of thoroughness, I will. What about the accusations against Tori? In your mind, is there any truth to them?"

"Honey, you and Tori have been dancing around each other for years. She likes you and she hasn't exactly been throwing herself at you like she's a whore. What makes you think she would be giving one of the witnesses sexual pleasure in an elevator? Don't be ridiculous! Tori is not that kind of woman. She's never been. She wouldn't go out with Derek Zane to advance her career and she sure as heck wouldn't compromise a case to please a man. That's the most stupid, ludicrous, insane thing I've ever heard. Trust me, working in this office, I thought I'd heard it all — until I heard that."

"I agree. I've known her for a long time. You can accuse her of being stubborn, hard-headed, passionate and fiery — but you can't accuse her of being unethical and reckless. Whoever is behind this has a personal axe to grind. Now I just have to figure out who and why."

"I'm so glad you're looking into it because everyone

else seems to think Tori did something wrong. I know that's not true. She's not perfect, but she certainly didn't do what she's accused of. Somebody needs to stand up for her because right now, she's not strong enough to fight for herself."

"I'll do my best, Crystal. I can't make any promises. But after so many years of fighting for justice for other people, somebody needs to fight for Tori."

"I think you're the perfect man for the job."

As much as I appreciate Crystal's faith in me I have to wonder if it's misguided. To put it mildly, this situation is a political hot potato. I'm not sure anyone else will be willing to be forthright and honest for fear of losing their jobs. Tori has some loyal friends and colleagues, but in cases like this I've often found that loyalty only goes so far when people are threatened with harm to their reputation or to their wallets.

They aren't the only ones at risk. If my CO knew what I was doing, he would be none too happy with my unofficial investigation. At this point, I'm operating under the assumption that what he doesn't know won't hurt him. Although, even as I think those thoughts, I know deep down what he doesn't know may actually end up hurting me. The captain frowns on off-the-books police work.

CHAPTER EIGHT

TORI

BONNI JEANNE COMES INTO my mom's bedroom as I'm in the middle of moving her bed and scrubbing the floor. "Hey, Cinderella, these are for you," she says as she sets the huge bouquet of roses down on the dresser.

"Boy, my mom has a lot more friends than I realized. She's been getting a ton of flowers and houseplants. This place is starting to smell like a nursery. Just put them on the kitchen table with the rest so I remember to change the water. I might swap them out with the flowers in her hospital room because those are gorgeous."

"No, I think you misunderstood me. These are not for Velma, these are for you."

"For me? Why would I be getting flowers? It's not my birthday."

"I don't know. Maybe you should read the card attached," Bonni Jeanne suggests with a wink as she takes the mop away from me.

Curious, I walk over to the dresser and smell the peach-colored roses and fish out the small note card. "Would you like to see if our timing is better this time?

Call me for details. ~ C.E."

Bonni Jeanne is practically stamping her foot with impatience as she asks, "Well? What does it say?"

I chew on my bottom lip for a moment before I answer, "I think I've just been asked out on a date."

"By whom?"

"A guy I've been flirting with for almost a decade," I explain with a wistful sigh.

"What are you waiting for? Most guys don't hang around that long!"

"That's a good question. I used to use the excuse that it would be a complicated thing with our jobs — you know, in case he ever got called as a witness and I'd have to explain our relationship. But, I guess that's not a valid excuse any longer."

Bonni Jeanne looks a little deflated. "Oh, you mean he's another attorney?"

"Oh good heavens no! Cody Erickson is a very hunky detective. He's one of those lethal guys who is both cute and wickedly smart."

"Sounds like you would be a fool to turn down a date with him."

"I've been called worse things lately," I retort with a grimace. "What about my mom?"

"Tori, you know you can't let your mom make you afraid to live your life. Your mom is in a rehab hospital where she'll be for quite some time until her hip heals. It's a locked, secure unit. They know all about her dementia and her propensity to roam. Velma is as safe as she'll ever be. Her leg is in traction. Go out and enjoy yourself."

"It seems wrong to go on a date when my mom is in

pain."

"If there is an upside to dementia, it's the fact that your mom doesn't have much awareness. The doctors are doing a good job of treating her pain. Since the surgery, Velma seems comfortable. You can forgive yourself for having a life even though she can't remember hers."

"Thanks, I needed to hear that. I'm going to call Cody. Our lives keep getting in the way of happiness. Maybe it's finally our turn this time."

Glancing around my newly marvelously clean house, I realize I can't put off this phone call any longer. I've run out of things to do to distract myself. Nervously, I dial Katie's phone number. A little detective work of my own unearthed it. When she picks up, I nervously spew the explanation I rehearsed. "Umm … Hi, is this Katelyn Ashford?"

"It isn't anymore, but it used to be. I'm Katie Anthony now, how can I help you?"

"I'm Tori Clarkson. I'm a friend of Cody Erickson."

"Oh, yeah, you're the prosecutor. You helped my friend Savannah Moore."

"I did. Well, I used to be the Assistant District Attorney, but that's a long story too. Anyway, I'm calling because I understand you used to be Cody's partner and you know him pretty well."

"Not as well as some — but, yeah I guess. Why?"

"Let me tell you a funny story. Cody and I have been friends for a long time. We've been trying to go out for almost as long. But life keeps getting in the way. Finally, he asked me out, but he doesn't want to screw it up. Now, he wants me to plan the date so I'll be happy with the outcome."

"That's downright devious. I have to hand it to Cody — he's made it so you can't blame him if the date goes poorly."

"Exactly. I thought it was quite clever. Unfortunately, I didn't realize how much stress it is on a guy to plan a date until I tried to do it myself. I have no idea what he likes. That's why I called you," I confess with a self-deprecating laugh.

"Ahh, what a perfect opportunity!" Katie practically squeals with glee.

"No, no!" I protest. "This is so not an opportunity for any pranks or revenge. I *want* this to be a good date. Cody and I have been trying to do this right for years and we keep missing. This could be a big chance."

"I'm sorry! Did you think I would mess that up for you? I'm trying to plot a way to completely knock his socks off. Cody has had a string of bad relationships. He's a little jaded. I'm not sure he believes dating can work for him. I think this is the perfect opportunity to show him how fun dating can be when you're with the right person."

"Oh … That's a lot of pressure. I'm not sure I'm even the right person for Cody. I have a lot of stuff going on in my life right now. I only agreed to go out with him because he was so sweet."

"But you like him, right?" Katie presses.

"I do. I like Cody a lot. I always have."

"Then, we have to pick a date which will completely

blow him away and remind him how incredible you are."

"How will we do that? I don't think dinner and a movie will cut it even if I spring for Junior Mints and a large bucket of popcorn."

"No, I have something a little bigger in mind. How do you feel about music?" Katie asks after a couple of beats of silence.

"I love it!"

"Any particular kind?"

"I like it all, but I'm partial to jazz."

"Hmm, we'll have to adjust our playlist, but I'm sure Declan can cover some jazz with no problem."

"Pardon me? I'm lost." I admit.

"Here's the deal — Aidan O'Brien and Tasha Keeley are doing an East Coast swing, so Logan and I can make an announcement to our families. We're doing a private VIP fundraising concert here with backstage passes to a dinner and dance to raise money for Hope's Haven."

"Sounds really fun — but I doubt Cody's dating budget would cover the cost of a private event."

"Don't even worry about it! There is not a snowball's chance in you know where I'd charge Cody to come to one of my gigs. It's because of his diligent training that I'm still alive. As far as I'm concerned, any event I work, he is welcome to come for free — and you are too, as his plus one."

"That's incredibly generous. When is your concert?"

"We'll be playing this next Saturday. We're renting one of the top floors of one of the major hotels in Gainesville — don't ask me which one. I can't remember the name of it right off the top of my head, but I'll text it to you. If the weather is nice, it'll be a rooftop concert."

"Wow, this seems like it was meant to be. Saturday was the day Cody wanted to go out. I guess it won't be Netflix and popcorn or going to see a movie he's already seen a million times, after all."

"I guess not. I love it when a plan comes together. I can't wait to see you again. I'm sure Cody will be over the moon."

"Okay, I'll touch base with you later. I'm sure I'll have a million and one questions."

"By the way, wear comfortable shoes. There will be dancing."

"Perfect! It's almost as if we planned it or something," I answer with a snicker in my voice, even though I'm sure it doesn't translate over the phone very well.

Bonni Jeanne glances over at Crystal as she sweeps back a section of my hair and clips it up. "What do you think? I think it looks elegant with the neckline of this dress."

Crystal claps her hands together. "Ooh, that's gorgeous — but how sturdy are those clips? She'll be dancing. We don't want her hair to fall down."

Bonni Jeanne arranges the back of my hair. "They work pretty well. I wore them to my niece's wedding and they stayed in all night."

I'm a little startled by my own reflection. "By the time you guys are done with me, Cody won't even recognize me. I hardly know me and I'm staring right at my glamorous self. Where did you get this dress, Crystal?"

"Before my daughter joined the military, she used to work at one of those high-end department stores. She had a bad habit of buying inventory right when it came in. Her closet is stuffed to the gills with clothes she never even got to wear." Crystal ties the belt tighter in the back.

"Are you sure it's all right for me to wear this? Maybe she was saving it for something," I ask.

"No honey, Jaclyn told me to donate all the stuff a long time ago. I never got around to it. So, consider yourself donated to. It looks beautiful on you. Jaclyn would be happy to see it being put to good use."

"This reminds me of the scene in Cinderella. I feel like I'm getting ready to go to some fancy ball instead of a concert," I say as I twirl around and look over my shoulder at my reflection in the mirror.

Bonni Jeanne smiles. "I think the dress is perfect for a concert. It's sexy and classy all at the same time."

I look down at the deep emerald colored sundress with buttons all the way up the back. "I can't believe the transformation. I've spent weeks in my workout clothes moping about being fired. I forgot what it's like to look sexy."

"You're not done yet," Bonni Jeanne says. "You need some knock-'em-dead lipstick."

I laugh out loud. "I don't think I have anything like that. It's not part of my usual courtroom garb."

Bonni Jeanne clears off some space on my dresser. "Don't you worry. My sister sells all this fancy makeup stuff. I have more samples than you can imagine."

"While you guys take care of lipstick, I'm going to go out to my car and get my jewelry trunk. Tori needs some earrings and I think I have some in my eighties drawer which will be perfect."

"Wait… What? You have a trunk just for your jewelry? You carry it around, and you have it sorted by decade?" I ask as my jaw drops wide open.

Crystal nods. "Well, honey, you said you were having a fashion emergency. Did you expect us to show up empty-handed?"

"I don't know! I thought you might bring a curling iron, an extra pair of pantyhose, and your favorite nail polish. I didn't know this would be like one of those makeover shows."

Bonni Jeanne lifts a huge case of makeup and places it on my dresser. She pulls out three shades of red lipstick. "Oh dear, is this too much for you? Are we making you nervous? We could go if you want us to —"

"No! I love that you guys dropped everything to come help me. I would be even more nervous if you weren't here. You guys are actually helping distract me. It's been forever since I've been on a date. I'm not even sure I remember how. I'm sorry, I just didn't expect all this pampering."

Crystal examines the lipsticks in Bonni Jeanne's hand. "Definitely go with the middle one. That one has a nice degree of sparkle and it's the perfect shade for Tori's beautiful skin tone. What do you think, honey? Isn't it beautiful?"

I raise an eyebrow. "It's a little bold."

"So are you," insists Crystal. "Tonight's the night for forgetting all of your problems and pretending to be someone you're not — someone with a bold and carefree spirit out to have a good time and leave her problems behind."

I grin. "You're right. When am I ever going to get an opportunity to be this carefree again? This is a once-in-a-lifetime opportunity. I might as well be bold. Like Bonni Jeanne said, let's knock his socks off."

Chapter Nine

Cody

Normally, I don't let anyone drive the 'Stang, but today is an exception. I didn't even flinch too much when I handed Tori the keys. Honestly, I was too distracted to think much about it.

Over the years, I've watched Tori grow from being simply another pretty girl to a stunningly beautiful woman as her confidence grew. There hasn't been a time I didn't think she was magnificent. Tonight, she's outdone herself. Her artfully applied makeup plays up the twinkle in her eyes as she refuses to tell me where we're going. My sister gets freaked out by the sound of the engine in my car; not so with Tori. She laughs with delight every time she has to shift the car into a new gear.

After a while, we pull up to one of the newest luxury hotels in Gainesville. To be honest, my heart skips a beat. I don't understand why we're here. If she wants to eat at the five-star restaurant, it's a little out of my budget. Okay, it's a *lot* out of my budget. Mentally, I'm going through my credit balances in my head to see if I can swing it without embarrassing myself. I breathe a sigh of relief when I realize that if I split the bill between credit cards, I can probably cover anything she would order. I'll probably have to do the stereotypical thing and order a salad — but, I can make it work.

When I look back over at Tori, I realize she's studying my reaction intently. "What's wrong? You look like you've seen a ghost."

"Uh … I'm just trying to figure out your game plan," I stammer awkwardly.

Tori shakes her head in dismay. "Whatever you're thinking, knock it off. I'm not who the rumors say I am. We're not here for that."

I put my hands up in protest. "I swear, that's not what I was thinking. I was trying to figure out if I could afford dinner. I've heard this restaurant is really expensive — a whole-day-of-pay kind of expensive."

Tori's skeptical expression softens as she responds, "I didn't even think about that. Lucky for you, that's not why we're here. Even if it was, if I found out about the prices, we would turn around and eat at Applebee's because I'm not that kind of person."

"Then why on earth are we here?" I press.

"It's a surprise. Wait in the car until I come around to get you. Then close your eyes," she instructs as she gets out of the car.

As I sit there waiting, I wonder what in the world I've gotten myself into — but it doesn't take long for her to appear on the other side of the car. She helps me out and instructs me to leave my eyes closed. "Relax, I used to work at a summer camp with people with visual impairments. I'm a superb guide."

"Look, I know I said you could plan the date, but isn't this taking it a little too far?" I ask in an exasperated tone.

"You'll be fine. You're a big brave officer of the law, remember?" she teases.

I reach out and feel her face before I pull her close for a scorching hot kiss. "Are you sure I can't talk you into another game? I'm sure we can come up with something more fun," I reply suggestively.

Tori backs away and puts her hand on my arm. "Umm … sorry … no. You agreed to play by my rules tonight. Besides, I want you to have the full experience," Tori teases as she carefully guides me into the hotel. I know we must look ridiculous, but Tori doesn't seem to care. I regret I ever agreed to this silly game because I want to watch her walk beside me. I know she looks magnificent. I didn't get a long enough look at her when we were walking toward the car, but I know her dress hugs her every curve like it was made for her.

I hear the elevator chime and we walk inside. I can sense other people are in the elevator, but no one is saying anything. I hear someone clear their throat and I don't think it's Tori. The elevator sounds again, and we exit the car and move down the hallway. I hear the sound of lots of voices. It's disconcerting for me not to be able to see what's going on and guard myself against any potential threat. Finally, my nerves get the best of me and I say to Tori, "Enough of this game. Please tell me what's going on. I don't like the direction this day is going."

"No cheating!" Tori insists. I feel cool hands cover my eyes as we enter a large room and the voices around me grow louder.

I hear rustling behind me and feel the hand slip off and change positions. Thinking Tori is about to fall on her high heels, I open my eyes and reach out to steady her. I'm confused when she's standing right beside me instead of behind mw.

Instinctively, I try to spin around. "What the he—"

"Now, is that any way to talk to your former partner?" Katie asks with a giggle.

"Katie Anthony? What are you doing here? I thought you were doing bodywork for some famous musicians —
"

Katie clicks her tongue at me. "My goodness … you must have lost your keen observational skills in your old age. Who exactly do you think you're here to see?"

I turn to Tori in shock. "You brought us to an Aidan O'Brien concert on our first date?"

She nods. "You said you wanted to dance. I figured you wouldn't mind a little live music."

"Mind? It's almost impossible to get tickets to see this guy. This is awesome!"

"So, you like it? Did I do a good job choosing our first date?" Tori asks with a hopeful grin.

I spin her around and plant a kiss on her lips, barely able to contain my excitement. "Abso-freaking-lutely! This is perfect. I couldn't have done it any better. No wonder you wanted to keep it a surprise," I respond after I reluctantly end our kiss.

She pulls my head down for another kiss before she remarks, "Huh … I guess you'll be really blown away by our VIP backstage passes. You don't have to worry about buying us dinner. We're having dinner with the band."

"No flipping way!" I exclaim, as I look around the room in wide-eyed amazement. "How in the world did you pull all this off?" Belatedly, I remember my former partner. "Where did Katie go?"

"She probably had to go back to work or maybe she's talking with her family. I think they're here tonight. She said something about sharing big news. We'll see them tonight at dinner."

"I was going to thank her for helping you plan this. It was kind of cheating, but you know what? I don't even care if you had Katie's help. However you did this, it's the best idea ever."

"I'm so glad I was able to pull off the surprise. All I can say is that I have a whole new level of respect for guys after planning all this. It's a lot harder than it looks. Let's go find our seats. Katie said she reserved spots up front for us."

Tori grabs my hand and leads me to the front of the room. I'm amused when I see a table with placards with my name next to Tori's. Apparently, Katie wanted to make sure I knew it was mine because in front of my chair is my favorite Starbucks drink and candy bar. Tori's eyes widen after she takes a sip of her drink. "I have no idea how she knows Horchata Almond milk Frappuccinos are my favorite. I didn't tell her — but she nailed it anyway."

"Her husband, Logan, works a lot with Tristan at Identity Bank. Together, they are righteously scary. It's a good thing they're the good guys. It would be frightening to contemplate what would happen if they were using their talents for evil."

From behind me I hear a loud snicker. "You are so funny, Cody. Of course, Tristan wouldn't be a bad guy. I don't think it's genetically possible. He loves dogs too much."

I spin around to see Darya's daughter sitting across the table from us. "Maya! Is that you? It can't possibly be! The Maya I know is a tomboy who is a world-class dog trainer. You're an elegant, miniature version of your mother." I turn to Tori. "You know Detective Darya Vick? This is her daughter Maya."

"You forgot, that's not my mom's name anymore. She changed it when she married Stuart. She's Darya Eastwood now. I think she sounds like a movie star."

Tori nods. "I've worked with Darya on several cases. She's a great asset to law enforcement." Tori smiles at Maya. "Hi, I'm Tori. I love your outfit. It's very vintage. Are you a fan of Aidan O'Brien?"

"I like his stuff okay. But I'm here to see Mindy Whitaker and Tasha Keeley-Hernandez."

"Honestly, I'm here to expand my music horizons, I don't know much about any of them, but my friend told me I would like them all. So, we'll see —" Tori admits with a grin.

"This is my first grown-up concert. I'm really excited."

"Are you here by yourself?" I ask as I look around for Stuart and Darya.

"I didn't drive myself, if that's what you're asking. I'm only thirteen. Mom and Dad are here somewhere. They're probably making out or doing something equally embarrassing — but they promised me they would pretend they didn't even know me today. As far as anybody knows, I'm just a fan here to see my favorite artists perform at a concert."

"You mean to tell me you didn't bring a date?" I

tease.

Maya wrinkles her nose and shakes her head vehemently. "Oh, no, not me! I like dogs a lot better than I like boys. Besides, Dad says I'm not allowed to date until I'm thirty-five. I'm not sure he's kidding."

Tori chuckles. "Stuart is an intense kind of guy under all his laid-back humor. There's a decent chance he may be serious. He does seem massively protective of the people he loves."

Maya shrugs. "Maybe someday, I'll think it's a bad thing. Right now, I think it's pretty cool. He does an awesome job of watching out for me and my baby sister. My mom is really happy."

Suddenly the house lights go down and Tasha and Jude appear at center stage. Jude takes the microphone. "We're doing something special tonight. We're here to raise money for Hope's Haven — an organization which provides training for search and rescue dogs and service dogs alike. But I understand we have a special fan in the audience who is new to our music. I understand she likes her music with a touch of soul. Throughout the night we'll be adding some cover songs to our usual playlist to make sure she feels comfortable here."

Tori looks at me in shock as if I had something to do with this development. I shrug and just join the rest of the audience in wild applause.

Jude continues as the spotlight zooms in on Tasha who looks surprisingly uncomfortable. "I'd like to give a shout out to my wife, Tasha. There was a time in my life I would've never been able to throw caution to the wind and toss new songs into the mix on a whim. Tasha taught me to believe in myself and the power of faith over fear.

I love her so much, and so will you. To start things off, let's do a little *Stand By Me* by the great Ben E. King."

Tori scoots close and leans against my chest as she holds my hand. I feel her softly inhale and exhale. "You're right. This is the most perfect date I've ever been on."

As we're waiting for dinner to be served, Maya is chatting away with her mom. "Mom! Did you see? Can you believe Mindy sang *Respect* with Tori, Cody, and me? It was like we were backup singers. I hope somebody got it on video because I want to show my friends. They'll never believe I was singing with a big star!"

Darya laughs out loud. "You have met your father, right? He's probably posted it online and tagged everyone he knows in this state … and fourteen others by now."

I cringe when I hear her say those words.

Darya sees my expression. "Oh no — I didn't even think about that. You're not working on anything undercover, are you?"

"Relax. If I was, I would've never set foot on the stage. I know people record stuff with their cameras. I'm not worried about me. Tori has received some bad press coverage recently. She doesn't need to be exposed to anymore bad publicity."

"Oh, I'm so sorry. I can ask Stuart to take it down. Just a minute, I'll go get him."

Tori reaches out to stop her. "Look, don't bother. Let Maya have her fun. The media is going to post negative stuff about me anyway." She looks down at her gorgeous dress. "At least today, I'm not wearing scroungy yoga pants and a T-shirt older than your daughter."

Darya smiles sympathetically. "Oh, I hear you. Every time they run a story about me, they pick the most god-awful shots of me. Everyone was shocked when they saw our wedding pictures. No one could believe I was actually photogenic because they've never seen a good picture of me."

"Tori looks magnificent tonight, but to be honest, I've never seen her look anything but beautiful," I comment as I lean down and kiss my stunning date on her cheek.

I wasn't prepared for my compliment to be met with a chorus of "Awws" from the females in the immediate vicinity of where we were sitting. The tips of my ears heat, and I take a gulp of ice water to cover my nerves.

Darya studies Tori intently. "I don't know if you know this, but Cody and I have worked together on several cases. Aside from my husband, I consider Cody to be one of the finest men I know. You are lucky to be dating him."

I clear my throat. "Umm, if you guys are planning to talk about me, maybe I should go find something else to do … because this is awkward."

Maya makes a dramatic show of whispering to me in a stage whisper, "It's supposed to be awkward, that's what makes it fun for them. They do it to me all the time."

"In that case, I think I'll go find a group of my friends to go talk to and leave you guys to your own devices," I tease.

"Not so fast Cody," Mindy says as she walks up to the table. "I need to talk to you guys."

I pick up a CD and show it to her. "We already bought the CD, see?" I joke. "No need to go in for the hard sell."

"This isn't about my career — although thanks for buying the CD. We're donating all the profits so Mitch can train more service dogs."

Tori moves her chair over and pulls one over from another table. "I really enjoyed the concert tonight. You guys were amazing. I was grateful you incorporated some of my favorite music into your set. Maybe you didn't do it for me, but I felt like you did."

Mindy grins at Tori. "Katie's one of my favorite people. She saved my life once. I know that Cody is one of her favorite people. From the looks of things, you mean a lot to Cody. It was the least we can do. If there's one thing we believe in around here, it's a good old-fashioned love story, even if we have to get there the hard way."

"I don't know if you'd call what Cody and I have an actual love story but he has been great during a really tough time."

"Remember that — because it's about to get tougher," Mindy advises in a somber tone.

Tori looks over at me with a puzzled expression as she grips my hand tighter. I shrug helplessly as I look to Mindy Francis. "I'm sorry I don't know what you mean."

Maya interrupts excitedly, "Oh, I bet I know! I read about this in an article about you. You're having one of your premonition thingies, right?"

Mindy nods tightly. "I am."

Darya stands to leave and grabs her daughter's hand. "Maybe we should give them a little privacy. As interesting as this is, it doesn't really have anything to do with us."

Mindy pins Darya with an intense gaze. "Actually, it does involve you and your daughter. Please stay."

Darya's hand trembles as she pushes her hair out of her face and sits back down. "Maybe Stuart should be here for this too," she whispers under her breath to no one in particular.

"Probably so," Mindy confirms quietly.

Darya doesn't even have to go get Stuart. As soon as he sees the stricken expression on her face, he sprints over to our table.

Without saying a word, Maya moves over a seat and makes room for her stepfather.

"Can somebody tell me why my wife looks like she's seen a ghost?" Stuart demands.

"Oh, probably because I'm rather ghostlike," Mindy answers.

"Mindy has premonitions when really bad things or really good things are going to happen. But, she can only tell us if it's a matter of life and death. Those are her rules. So, it must be something pretty bad," Maya explains before Mindy has a chance.

Darya whips her head around and looks at Mindy skeptically. "Is this true?"

"Yeah, that's a startlingly accurate summary of what happens with me," Mindy confirms. "The only thing Maya left out is that I only see a portion of what's happening. I don't always see the whole scene. I see bits and pieces. So, I can give you what I've got — but it's up to you to interpret it. People have described it as a terrible riddle which makes no sense at first. If that's the case here, I apologize in advance, but I'm doing the best I can."

" Must be frustrating for you," Stuart remarks.

Mindy nods. "I agree, but I guess it's like my husband says. Even a little information is more helpful than none at all."

"I suppose that's true," I comment. "What do you have for us?"

"Those who are missing? You'll find them on YouTube pretending to be those who they are not."

Darya and I look at each other with wide eyes. "Did you check YouTube?" I ask.

"I found none on my caseload. Facebook and Snapchat, sure, but no YouTube channel. What about you?"

"My victim was grounded from the Internet for sneaking out with her boyfriend. At the time she disappeared, she had no social media accounts. Our forensic people found nothing on her phone or her iPad."

Maya shifts uncomfortably in her chair. I notice the change in her countenance immediately. "Maya, what's up?"

She sends a furtive glance in her parents' direction before she answers, "I think I know what you're talking about. Last year, before summer break we had an end-of-the-year talent show. I brought Atlas to school and showed off his agility skills. I didn't win a prize or nothing. Those went to the singers and the guy who played his guitar really great — like so great he could be part of Mindy's band. Anyway, the principal asked me what I wanted to be. I said I'd like to have my own TV show about dog training someday."

Stuart nods. "We've talked about this, I think that's a great idea."

"That's not the creepy thing. The next day, there was a note in my locker. It was an offer to make me a YouTube star. It told me to call this number but not from my own cell phone. I was supposed to use a public phone like at the library or buy a special throwaway phone which couldn't be traced."

"Maya! Why didn't you bring the note to me?" Darya exclaims. "That's the kind of crime the police department investigates. You know, that's my job —"

Maya shrugs. "I didn't figure it was any big deal. Actually, I thought it was some mean girls playing a prank on me, so I threw it away. I didn't even call the number because it was just too weird."

"Well, I'm glad you trusted your instincts," I praise. "Do you know if any of the rest of your friends got notes like that?"

Maya tearfully shakes her head. "I don't know. I didn't know it was a big deal. I should've said something. I'm so sorry. Now those kids are missing, huh? Is it my fault?"

"No, Maya, it's not your fault the kids are missing. We're not exactly sure why they're missing. But if someone took them, it's the fault of whoever took them," Tori corrects gently.

Maya looks up at Mindy. "Are those kids dead because of me?"

Mindy shakes her head. "None of this is because of you and as far as I can tell, no one is dead — yet." She turns to me. "Time is of the essence. You need help —

someone who can think like the bad guys. I think you need Tobias Payne. Tell Tristan you need him here yesterday."

"Okay, I'll jot down his name and I'll give Tristan a call and tell them what you said," I reply as I pat my pockets looking for my ever-present notebook.

Tori taps me on the shoulder. "I don't think you'll need to do that. Tristan is standing right over there."

"Oh, okay," I respond, feeling unsure about what I should do next. This was intended to be a grand date, aimed at forgetting all of our problems. I'm not supposed to be working, but as a cop, I'm never really truly off duty. My mind is always spinning and working on my cases, whether I want to be or not.

Tori must sense my indecision. "Go. Your first priority is those kids. We can have a perfect date another time. We have to save those kids. Who knows what's happening to them and their families are waiting for them."

Mindy sighs. "Sometimes, I hate my gift. Especially when I know it will completely disrupt people's lives."

"Mindy, you can't think that way. You gave us a lead when we were totally out of leads. If it turns out to be right, you might've saved at least four lives, if not more. It sounds like whoever this is may have been casting a far wider net than we ever anticipated. There could be dozens and dozens of children missing that law enforcement hasn't been aware of before."

Tori removes her dangling earrings and sticks them in her purse. "That's what I'm afraid of." She glances over at Mindy. "I hope you understand that suddenly I'm not very hungry. I have other priorities. We have to get our heads around the scope of this case and how the information you just gave us fits into what we already know."

"Tori, I know you're hungry. I heard your stomach growl," Mindy discloses pointedly. "I'll ask the kitchen to box up your dinners so you can take them with you to wherever you're planning to work."

Impulsively, Tori stands up and gives Mindy a hug. "Thank you for what you do, it can't be easy."

"If it saves those kids, it's worth it. By the way, hang in there. I know it's hard to do the right thing. Just remember people who do things for political recognition and ill-gotten financial gain are like a flash in the pan. Their true colors will bleed through and their allies will be exposed. Stay true to yourself."

Mindy's words bring tears to Tori's eyes. In a voice choked with emotions, she says, "Thank you for the reminder."

"Remember, Cody is on your team even when his job makes it seem like he's not. Balance is the key. I'm sorry to cut this short, but you guys need to go."

Chapter Ten

Tori

I'm used to Cody exuding nothing but quiet confidence. However, as we wait in the terminal at Jacksonville International Airport for Toby Payne to arrive, he's a nervous wreck. His knee is bouncing a million miles an hour as he consults the reference pictures of the missing teenagers and surfs through hundreds of pages of YouTube sites looking for matches.

I slide a fresh cup of coffee in front of him as I cautiously ask, "Don't you have a computer forensic team at your disposal to do that kind of thing?"

Cody looks up at me with a slightly dazed expression as he struggles to focus his tired eyes. "Technically, yes. However, they're incredibly backed up. Even if I sent this to them as a priority, it would still take them weeks to get to it. We don't have weeks to find these kids, we have hours."

I pull my iPad out of my purse and sit on the stool across from Cody. "Okay, I understand. Two pairs of eyes are better than one. Tell me how you're approaching this. YouTube is a wasteland of random information."

"Remember a couple of weeks ago when I went back and re-interviewed the families? I was looking for connections between the kids. So, I asked about social media and whether they had any hobbies. For example, DeAndre is involved in the skateboarding community, so I'm searching YouTube channels about boarding to see if he pops up there."

"Wow! Makes sense, but so daunting. There has to be a better approach."

"I think that's why Mindy suggested we bring in Toby Payne. He is supposed to be a phenom on the computer. His specialty is programming and social media. As a teenager, he spent several years as a missing child. He knows how the predators work. Hopefully, he can give us some insight into that too."

I pick up a piece of paper off of the stack he is working on. "Okay, I guess I'll work on Tallulah Johnson. She is strikingly beautiful. She should be easy to spot if we're lucky."

Cody nods. "Tallulah's passions are theater and journalism. She already has a scholarship to go to college. She's done some on-camera work for a local cable station. Her mom said she used to sing in the church choir all the time. So, you might find some music videos out there or maybe some student interviews."

I look at the clock on my iPad. "When is Toby's plane due in?"

Cody glances at his military type watch. "It should be anytime now."

"That's good news. As far as I'm concerned, help can't arrive fast enough."

Toby puts his luggage in my mom's room. It's not really my mom's room anymore. I just call it that because old habits are hard to break.

I've made the decision with the doctors to place my mom in specialized care where they can better handle her dementia and the problems caused by her broken hip. It was sad and difficult, but probably the best decision for everyone. Bonni Jeanne found a different client to work with and she is much happier. She is taking care of a quadriplegic student and attends classes with him during the day, but still lives with me at night to save on living costs. I'm more than okay with our new arrangement. Bonni Jeanne has become like family.

"I can't tell you how much I appreciate this. It's Tristan's habit to put us up in luxury hotels. But after all the time I spent on the run as a teenager, I can't stand staying in them, even very nice ones. This means the world to me."

"It's not a problem. I have this nice old house and lots of space. Thank you for coming all the way across the United States to help Cody with his case."

"Everyone deserves to be found. It's as simple as that."

"I agree —"

I'm cut off by the sound of the doorbell.

"Oh, that's Cody. Come with me, we'll get set up in the dining room. I added power strips, so we can plug in all the computer equipment there."

"Perfect. I brought a bunch. If you work with Tristan

much, you know he likes to deck us out."

I rush to the door and greet Cody with a brief hug. "I really like Toby. He's such a serious young man. I have a hunch he totally knows his stuff," I whispered in Cody's ear as we walked toward the dining room.

When Cody sees what Toby is setting up, he laughs out loud. "I can see you have a lot in common with Jameson. I worked with your brother a time or two before he moved to Oregon. He has a passion for gadgets too."

Toby grins widely, in the first genuine smile I've seen from him since we met yesterday. "There's a reason I idolize my big brother. Who do you think taught me everything I know?"

Cody adds a laptop to the mix. "I borrowed this from the department. It has all the files and information we've got on each case. I have permission from the department to share this information with you because you work for Identity Bank and we contract with your company."

Toby looks at me and blushes. "What about her?" Obviously, he's heard the rumors.

Cody smiles slyly. "Funny thing about that — my captain gave me permission to hire as much temporary help as I need to process this case and expedite things. He said I have permission to hire anybody I wish to handle the clerical end of things as long as they could pass the department criminal background check. So, I used your company to run a check on Tori. Just as I expected, her record is clean as a whistle."

He turns and hands me a contract. "Victoria Clarkson, I am hereby offering you a position as a project assistant on this investigation. You'll be doing clerical tasks and research as well as other tasks as assigned. The pay is nominal, but the reward is potentially great if we locate the missing children. Do you accept?"

"Normally, I would be concerned this would mess up my attempt to go after my employer for wrongful termination, but at this moment, my concern for the missing teens takes precedence." I take the paper from him and sign it.

"Wow, you didn't even take time to read it," Toby observes. "For all you know, he could be signing you up for a lifetime of indentured servitude."

I stand on my tiptoes and brush a kiss across Cody's cheek. "Nope, not this guy. He is as honorable as the day is long. I trust Cody to look out for my best interests."

"I knew there was a reason I hired you," Cody answers with a wink.

I blush before I put a collage of all four pictures of the kids up on my big screen TV above the dining room table and turn to Toby. "What do you need from us? How can we best help you do your job?"

"I reviewed the notes you sent — thanks for that, by the way. I'm not sure I understand your process. Are you trying to match the teen's faces by reviewing social media sites by hand?" Toby asks incredulously.

"We are. Our computer forensics lab has a case backlog several months long. We figured doing something was better than doing nothing," Cody answers with a grimace.

"Oh man … I wish you would've called Tristan in on this sooner. A few years ago, he developed software to match faces. He uses it to help prevent identity theft and catfishing. It would be ideal for filtering through YouTube videos and social media sites to help find your missing kids."

"How precise do the search parameters need to be? We haven't quite nailed down everyone's hobbies the perpetrator might have targeted. Will that make the search more difficult?" I ask.

"Yes and no. The computer doesn't actually care about the parameters when it's searching through pictures. It's a matter of volume. The more pictures it looks at, the longer the comparisons will take — but, it doesn't make it more difficult. It just makes it more time-consuming."

"How much more time consuming?" Cody presses. "Mindy made it sound like speed was critical."

"This is impossible for me to determine. I don't know how good your information is or how specific your searches might be. I know nothing about your Internet connection. It could be eight hours or it could be a day and a half."

"Since we live so close to the university, they came through a few years ago and put fiber-optic lines in. My Internet service is quite fast here. I upgraded to the fastest service available when I was practicing law. I tend to be a little inpatient when I'm doing case research."

"Okay, that'll help." Toby says as he rapidly types information into his computer. "Hopefully, the wide searches won't add too much time. Who knows, we could luck out and hit pay dirt right up front."

I watch him type for a few minutes. It's awe-inspiring. I thought my paralegals type quickly, but they have nothing on him. Eventually, my curiosity gets the best of me and when his fingers leave the keyboard, I ask, "Are you going to run the searches simultaneously?"

"Eventually," Toby says with a nod. "There's a chance these kids are being held together. So, they might be featured in the same pictures. However, I want to search for the child who has been missing the longest first. We'll add the next longest missing child and so on until we have them all in the system."

A shiver travels up my spine as I realize how cavalier our conversation must seem as we are casually discussing the fate of four terrified children. "Do you really think whoever has them is holding them together?"

"At this point, your guess is as good as mine. One of the reasons it took people so long to find me is that people expected my kidnapper to behave in a logical manner. Everything about her was illogical. She would do things which were completely baffling. Some of them were to elude capture — I'll give you that. But most of the things she did were just because she was totally crazy and had more than a few screws loose. We can think we understand what this person might do and try to make a move or two ahead of him, but there are no guarantees our guesses will be right."

"How do you suggest we focus our search, if we can't do it based on common sense?" Cory asks, His voice rising with frustration.

"Don't get me wrong, I'm not saying throw logic out the window. I'm just cautioning against relying on it too much," Toby explains. "You don't want to exclude the randomness of illogical people. So, I would put as much information about each victim as we possibly can but I would also broaden the search out to include all YouTube videos and other social media sites. I'll focus on the sites which mirror YouTube but don't exactly follow the rules."

I sigh. "Geez, as if finding four needles in the haystack of all social media isn't complicated enough, now we've got to be worried about imposter sites too?"

"Yeah, it's part of what makes my job a challenge."

"In this case, I wish you didn't have a job at all, but since you do, I wish it wasn't quite so challenging."

"You and me both. I wish we lived in a world where no one ever needed to be found," Toby says wistfully. "But, since there are still people missing, we need to get to work."

"Sounds good. I am ready to have something concrete to do. I feel like I've been spinning my wheels," Cody admits. "Tell us what to do — we are at your disposal."

"I've modified the user interface to Tristan's program for our purposes. I've created a template to ensure that we build a complete profile on each missing teenager. I replicated the form on Google forms so each of you can use it. When you've finished entering the information on the case assigned to you, you can forward the information to me and I will run it through Tristan's program."

"Should we do this in any order?" I ask as I gather up the files.

"Which teen has been missing the longest?" Toby asks.

"Isadora López, age fifteen has been missing since New Year's Day. She was supposed to meet some friends to play soccer, and she never showed."

"I won't ask you if she had problems with her family or her boyfriend. It was questions like that which led people to draw all sorts of wrong conclusions about my family and my case," Toby has to stop and draw in a deep breath before he continues. "The police thought they knew what was happening to me — when in actuality, they had no clue. They thought they knew what I was all about based on my age and what they thought was going on in my family. They couldn't have been more wrong if they tried. So, we're *not* going to make any of those guesses about these kids. Chances are if we did, they would be wrong."

"I'm so sorry. I feel like I need to apologize for my whole profession. Sometimes we get stuck in a rut of what we've always done. We believe it should be done that way, whether or not it works. I know I'll never look at a case the same way again now that I've heard it from your perspective," I reply as my voice breaks. I pause to take a drink of my coffee and collect my emotions. I glance over at Cody and he seems as shaken as me.

"Toby, after all this is done and we find this group of missing kids and lock up those responsible, I want you to help me revamp the way we do things in our department. I handle training rookies. I don't want to merely train them to do it how it's always been done. I want to train my officers to find the missing people in the least amount of time possible. I think you can help me do that."

"I'd be honored to turn my nightmare into a positive for other people."

CHAPTER ELEVEN

CODY

I TRY TO DISGUISE a yawn as I drive up to the prosecutor's office. Toby, Tori and I didn't finish inputting information into the computer until very early this morning. Breaking down the lives of four vibrant teenagers to bits and bytes the computer understands is painstaking business.

I thought I understood Toby's story from all the news accounts and what little I had heard from Jameson and Tristan. I was wrong. Last night, over the course of several hours, as we dissected the lives of four seemingly unrelated teenagers and discussed how a predator might approach them, shards of Toby's story began to emerge — stories of how he went from an innocent, talented gaming phenom to a hostage who flew under everyone's radar for years. He told stories of how he was initially fooled into thinking his predator was his friend, only to find out she was anything but. He shared how he learned to fend for himself after his captor became addicted to drugs and completely mentally unstable.

Honestly, I don't know how a teenage boy takes a fun habit like playing on computers and turns it into a way to support himself and his kidnapper while still staying hidden from the world because he believed his kidnapper would kill his family if he said anything. It must've been horrific. I can't help but wonder if the missing kids are facing similar challenges.

Every second which ticks by feels like an eternity. After I pull into the parking lot of the government building, I check my phone for what seems like the hundredth time. I curse under my breath when I don't see a new message from Toby. I barely refrain from sending him another message when I reread the last message from him. *"I can't make the computers process any faster. It is what it is. I'll let you know what I find as soon as I have a result. Chill. Don't you have more productive things to do than watching your phone?"*

I sigh. The kid may be a decade younger than me, but he has a point. I grab the hot pizza from the backseat of my car and carefully pick up the bakery box with my other hand. I plaster a smile on my face as if I have no other worries in the world.

Grinning, I start singing at the top of my lungs as I theatrically wish Crystal a happy birthday. At first, I'm putting on my smile — but after I see the look of shock on my friend's face, my smile becomes genuine. "What in the world are you doing here?" she gasps.

"Is it, or is it not, your birthday?"

"It is … I guess," she stammers.

"Well, then it should be perfectly obvious what we're doing here — we're having a party," I announce.

"Is that pizza I smell?" a tall, willowy redhead asks as she saunters out of what used to be Tori's office.

She walks over to Crystal's desk where I set the pizza

down and lift the lid. She groans out loud when she sees I've ordered Crystal's favorite pizza. "Oh my gosh! Deep-dish sausage and pepperoni pizza. That's so against my Keto diet, I don't even want to think about it. It's like pure torture."

I stick my hand out for her to shake. "Hi, I'm Cody Erickson. Pizza delivery guy a.k.a. party planner and a friend of Crystal. Haven't you heard, any junk food you eat at a party has no calories in it? Those are the rules — or, at least that's what my sister always tells me."

"Look at you! You're just adorbs," she says in a high-pitched voice like she's in a play. "You're cute and funny too." Her tone changes pitch and she says, "Hello, my name is Stacy Hildabrand. I'm the lead prosecutor here."

I don't have to feign surprise as I say, "Wow! You don't look old enough to have that kind of position. You must have graduated from Yale or Harvard ... or one of the other Ivy League schools."

She giggles like a cartoon character. "Oh, I wish. No, I went to school at John Marshall."

"Still, that's nothing to sneeze at. I've heard they're pretty competitive. Your LSAT scores must've been impressive."

"Not really. It helps when your grandfather gives a lot of money to the law library. I was a legacy student."

"Still, you landed an impressive position like this — " I say with a raised eyebrow. "You're young. You must have an impressive track record to advance so quickly."

Stacy averts her gaze when she notices Crystal studying her. She shrugs. "I guess some people are just luckier than others. You know, sometimes it's who you know rather than what you know. My family is well connected, if you know what I mean. I've been pretty good at … umm … networking."

Underneath her breath, Crystal mumbles, "Yeah, I just bet."

"You know, it's weird. I have been in law enforcement for a long time and I've never heard of you coming up through the ranks. Usually, I do."

Stacy blushes to the roots of her hair. "I like to work the back channels."

Crystal breaks into a fit of coughing behind me. "Oh, that reminds me; I left the soda in my car. It sounds like you could use something to drink, Crystal. Would you like to come help me with the plates and napkins?"

When she regains her composure, Crystal looks at me with complete befuddlement but agrees, nonetheless. We walked to my car in silence, but once we're hidden behind my trunk lid, she hisses at me, "What are you doing here? Tori told me you guys are elbow deep in a case — a *really* important case. Why are you surprising me for my birthday — which by the way — isn't until next Saturday?"

I pat Crystal on the shoulder. "You, my dear, are serving as my cover. Think about it. If it were not for you would I have any reason to come talk to Stacy Hildabrand?"

Crystal chews on her fingernail for a moment. "I guess not. I wish you didn't have to. That woman isn't worth the time you take away from your other case."

"Maybe not. But getting to the bottom of why this happened is worth it. Besides, at the moment, we're at a standstill on the other case until the specialized computers do their magic. So, I might as well try to figure out why my girlfriend got screwed seven ways to Sunday by the agency she was loyal to for almost a decade."

Crystal crosses her arms in front of her and sets her jaw. "Okay, but do you have to be so nice to Stacy? It makes you seem like a traitor."

"You don't have to worry about where my loyalties lie. I'm squarely in Tori's corner. I have been for a really long time — but I'm even more firmly planted there now. But … yes, I have to be nice. It's how the job is done. It's called being a professional. Don't take it personally. I've been nice to murderers and pedophiles too. It doesn't mean I side with them. It merely means I'm doing my job."

Crystal shakes her head and chuckles. "Okay, I guess I'm being a little dramatic. Stacy isn't so bad. But I still don't like her — she's not Tori, and the job isn't rightfully hers."

"I hear you. Let's go back in and have some pizza and soda and see if we can get Stacy to talk a little more about how she ended up with Tori's job. I know it's hard — but I need you to dial back the hostility. Maybe if she thinks she's among friends, she'll open up more and give us insight about how someone as green in the field as she is could land the top prosecutor's position."

"Well, I have a hunch, but if I said it out loud, my mama would wash my mouth out with soap," Crystal snipes.

"Okay, for today, we'll table those theories and just listen to what Stacy has to say. Who knows, she could collaborate your theory."

"Oh, for her sake, I hope not. My theory doesn't put her in a very good light."

"I know this is awkward, but remember the primary purpose is to rebuild the opportunity to gain evidence for Tori."

As Crystal walks by me with her arms loaded with paper plates, plastic cutlery and a tube of plastic cups, she elbows me. "Okay, as difficult as it is for me to be civil under the circumstances, I will remember to keep my eye on the prize and not get distracted."

"Tori said I could count on you. She said nothing goes on in this office you don't know about, and I should trust your opinion implicitly."

"See, I miss those kind of smarts. I pray every night we can unravel this ball of yarn and get Tori back on the job where she belongs."

"Me too. In the meantime, we have to go on a fact-finding mission while we throw you a birthday party. After all, there's pizza in there, just calling our names."

As I'm loading up the car after my carefully orchestrated impromptu birthday party, my cell phone buzzes in my pocket. I pull it out and look at it with great trepidation. I've been holding my breath metaphorically for so long I'm almost afraid to look. *Holy crap! It is a message from Toby.* "Meet me at Identity Bank ASAP!"

For once, I'm glad I'm driving a department vehicle instead of my beloved Mustang. I'm not even sorry when I flip on the siren to maneuver around a slow-moving vehicle after I leave the parking lot. It's too bad I can't share this development with Tori. It's one thing to have her on my official payroll as my assistant. It's quite another to subject her to the scrutiny of all my coworkers considering all the gossip that's going in the papers. I'd just rather not. Hopefully, we'll have something to celebrate later.

When I left the house this morning, she had a bad headache. She blamed it on focusing on the computer screen too much. Even so, I wonder if the stress of everything is getting to her.

John is waiting for me in the lush reception area at Identity Bank. "How did you know it was me?" I ask him. We've been friends for years, but the things he can accomplish with his visual impairment never cease to amaze me.

"For one thing you always keep your keys and your change in your left front pocket. Most people carry them in their right pocket. Secondly, you have a weird hitch in your gait."

"Not much gets past you — no wonder Tristan hired you. I'm left-handed, that's why my keys and my change is in the other pocket. And a few years back one of the bad guys shot me in the ankle while they were trying to get away. The therapist told me I did a great job with my rehab — but apparently not good enough for you."

"Tristan and Toby are waiting for you in conference room C. If you'll follow Tuffy and me, we'll show you the way," John says as he gives Tuffy's harness a microscopic tug.

When we walk into the conference room, I'm relieved to see Isadora's picture up on the big screen with a big orange tag on it which says Possible Match.

"What did you find, Toby?"

"*I* didn't find anything. This break is all due to the

face recognition software. It found an 89% match.”

“Is that considered good?”

“Under the circumstances, with the lighting challenges and the way teenagers change almost daily, I think so,” Toby replies as he continues to type things into the computer.

I look up at Tristan. “Do you concur?”

“It looks like a solid lead. I’ve got other programs trying to trace the IP address so we can get a physical location where this was posted from.”

“What kind of video is it?”

“Not what we expected,” Toby admits. “It has nothing to do with soccer. It’s a video about painting kids’ faces for Halloween or birthday parties. It turns out that Isadora is a talented artist as well as a gifted athlete. The videographer appears to be one of the children whose face is being painted. The video is shaky and not professional quality but there were enough shots of Isadora’s face that the face recognition software was able to identify her.”

“Has anyone notified her family?” I ask as my heart races.

“Not yet,” Tristan replies. “As much as I trust my program, I'd much prefer we have human eyes on our victim to confirm the identity first before we get anyone’s hopes up.”

“I agree. That would be a safer plan but how long will it take your program to find out where she actually is? Will we need to subpoena YouTube to get the records? That will take a while, won’t it? I suppose we could get a search warrant based on exigent circumstances. I don’t know how old this video is, but Isadora has been missing since New Year's —"

"Identity Bank is going to try to get all this with information publicly available using our extensive resources," Tristan answers.

"Sorry, I'm just thinking out loud here, trying to puzzle it through. Our first priority is to get Isadora home safe, but we also owe it to her to capture whoever did this to her."

"We're on the same page here. Toby and I are working on it right now. We still have three other missing teens. What we don't know is if their disappearances are related to Isadora's, or if they are completely separate. So, when we go chasing after the bad guys in Isadora's case, we need to be careful to protect not only her but make sure there aren't more potential victims."

I smirk at Tristan. "Did you just politely tell me to cool my jets and let you do your job? I can't tell you how many times I've told victims that very same thing. I've never been on the receiving end of that lecture. It feels a little strange, to be honest."

"I imagine it does — but unless you think getting a search warrant based on the YouTube video is a faster process than what we're doing here, there isn't a lot you can do until the computer finishes its process and pops out an address for us."

"Have I mentioned how much I hate waiting?" I grouse.

"Several times!" Toby and Tristan answer in unison.

"I understand waiting sucks. Do yourself a favor, take your girlfriend out for a nice lunch. Once this case starts rolling, you two may not have a chance to come up for air," Tristan replies.

I sigh as I glance at my watch impatiently. "I wish I could disappear with Tori and not come up for air for a while — but I have a hunch that's not what you meant."

"Not this time. But if you guys can ride out the storms that are coming your way, eventually you can celebrate your love story like that. You can be like Rogue and me. We like to fly to Paris on a random Tuesday just for fun."

"Well, it can never be said you don't dream big, Tristan. I think we all would like to follow in your footsteps."

Chapter Twelve

Tori

From our corner booth at Reggae Shack Cafe, I glance around the packed restaurant. It has become our favorite getaway since we discovered we both crave its spicy Caribbean food. We eat here so often they don't even bother to hand us menus anymore. When they see us come to the door, they just turn in an order for us and serve our drinks.

"I can't believe we were able to coordinate our lunch schedules today." I comment with a contented sigh as I drink my fresh fruit smoothie. "I have been in meetings with my mom's doctors all day. Her new medicine is helping with the dementia but it's causing other side effects. So, they're trying to figure out whether it's worth the risk. I hope they keep her on it though. She actually knew who I was today, and we had a great conversation. She remembered my law school graduation. I couldn't bring myself to tell her I'm not practicing law anymore," I admit as I blink back tears.

Cody squeezes my hand.

"Hopefully, that's just a temporary bump in the road."

"That would be nice, but they've already put someone in my job — doesn't look so temporary to me."

"Yes, I've met Stacy. Even she admits she got the job through 'back channels'. She made no secret she didn't get her position based on skill," Cody says, grinning like a Cheshire Cat.

I roll my eyes so hard they can see last Tuesday. "Uh-huh, welcome to the legal profession. That's pretty much standard operating procedure. It's hardly a smoking gun, Detective Erickson."

"By itself, maybe not — but somebody wanted her in that position and you out. So, if we look at the intersection of those two things. Maybe we'll find the person with the motive to do you harm."

"I'm a prosecutor. I put people in jail. I'm an aggressive black woman who got promoted over some people who were not minorities and who were less qualified. Take your pick. Not to sound dramatic, but I probably have more than a few people I've ticked off over the years. People aren't beating down my door or anything to get at me, but they're probably cheering for my demise in the privacy of their offices."

"It might seem like the list is huge — but I've got it whittled down to just a few suspects. In a couple of weeks, I should be able to pin it down even further."

"Okay … let's say you're successful. Then what? It's unlikely anyone will do anything about it in this political environment. Derek Zane wants to give the impression that he's the perfect District Attorney and he runs a tight ship. Do you think he'll pursue an investigation of his own shop?"

Cody is silent for a couple of moments as he

considers what I said. "Depending on what I find, I could open an official investigation and then ask for an outside investigator from a different county or maybe on a state level."

"I appreciate the thought — but it wouldn't work. Anybody with two eyes could figure out we're dating now and that you have a personal motive in trying to figure out what's going on. You're not exactly an uninterested law enforcement type now."

Cody grins. "When it comes to you, I've never actually been an 'uninterested law enforcement type'."

"True. But now it's totally obvious. Anyone could pick up on your bias."

"So, you're just going to give up? I got news for you … I'm not sure your replacement understands Black's Law Dictionary isn't a shade of her favorite mascara. Are you willing to just hand over your legacy to her?"

"No! I didn't hand over my legacy to anyone. It was stolen from me!" I snap.

Cody runs his fingers down my cheek. "I know things have been tough with your mom and you have had little chance to fight this. But now you've got a whole team of people helping with your mom and … you've got me, Crystal and Bonni Jeanne in your corner. Don't let the creeps, known as your former bosses, get away with this. We've got your back."

"Do you think I can actually fight the whole system? They've destroyed my reputation."

"The people who know you, I mean *really* know you, know you are better than that. Go show the rest of the world who you really are."

I flash him a watery smile. "Crystal and Bonni Jeanne

make a phenomenal makeover team, but I'm not sure the four of us can take on the whole system and win."

Cody gets up from the table and holds his hand out to me. When I grasp it he pulls me to a standing position. For several moments, he simply stares at me. Then he draws me in closer for a hug. As he's holding me tight, he insists, "We won't know until we try. Besides, it's not just us. You've got Katie, Tristan, Mitch, Jessica, Darya, Stuart and Maya — not to mention everyone else in our circle." He pulls away and kisses me gently on the lips. He smiles encouragingly. "You haven't even met everybody yet."

"It's not like I've had a lot of free time," I mutter, shaking my head in frustration.

Cody hugs me one more time and then turns his chair around backwards and sits down on it. "We're like a freakin' army of tattooed, tamale-eating, do-gooders. The bad guys won't have a clue what hit them."

"You're saying everybody will join my fight just because I ask them to — no questions asked?"

"Will they step up to the plate if I ask? Absolutely. With no questions? Probably not. This is a chatty, invasive bunch — in a good way. They want to be supportive, so they want to know what's going on with you. Don't be surprised if they pick your brains and try to figure out how they can help you. But they will be helpful. I've seen this group pull together in amazing ways."

"Now that I think about it, so have I. I've seen your friends support Savannah when she had to testify against the guy who held her hostage, Mick Ricard, and then again when she had to repeat the process with the Brennans."

"Don't forget what happened when Katie was chased

across the country by a deranged stalker," Cody adds.

"That's right I heard about that. Didn't her stalker mess with someone's wedding?"

"Yeah, the scumbag sure did. It was Katie's. I promised her I wouldn't call the police. But we had to. Katie does nothing in a small way — two ceremonies, two call-outs."

I snicker. "Well, when you put it that way, I guess my drama fits right in with everyone else."

"Like I said, we've dealt with all sorts of crazy stuff in our group. We're used to supporting people through thick and thin. Just let us know what we can do."

"Before I can tell you how you can help me, I have to decide how I'm going to move forward. I've been stuck for so long. I don't know what to do next."

"I didn't mean to put pressure on you, whatever you decide, I'll support your decision."

"Really?" I ask skeptically. "You'd really support me if I decide to do nothing?"

Cody shrugs. "I've always said you're one of the smartest people I know. If you decide the best thing for you is to let the matter drop, I trust your judgment that you're doing the best thing for you and your family — even if I would've made a different decision."

For several moments I am too stunned to speak.

"Is something wrong?" he probes when the silence becomes uncomfortable.

I take a deep breath. My thoughts are racing in my mind and it's difficult to verbalize them. Finally, I let out my breath and decide to be brutally honest. "You and I have been doing this dance around each other for years.

You've told me many times how much you like me. I guess I didn't realize until this moment how much you meant it."

"Of course, I like you. I like you a lot. Did you think I was kidding?"

"No, not exactly — but what you said to me about respecting my decision even if you disagreed with it is probably the single nicest thing anyone has ever said to me. You've given me a lot to think about."

Cody looks incredulous. "That's it? You're just going to leave me hanging?"

"Not exactly. I can safely admit that I like you too."

Things were weird when Cody dropped me off after lunch. He seemed to hope I could give him a definitive statement about what I was planning to do. Although he says he'll be supportive either way, I think being in limbo is difficult for him.

To make matters worse, the cases of the missing teens seem to be stuck in neutral as well. Every time there's a little progress, everything comes to an abrupt stop as he has to wait for the computers to spit out more information for him to act on.

I can't say I'm in much better shape. I tossed and turned all night as I tried to come up with a game plan. Finally, I decided I had to have at least one conversation to clarify things. It's a conversation I should've had months and months ago. Instead, I let my circumstances overwhelm me.

I walk up to Derek's office and knock on the door. As always, I'm amazed by the opulence. Even when I was officially his assistant district attorney, I never figured out why he felt he needed to be separated from the rest of the prosecutors who work for our county. He's supposed to be the head of our team. The operative word being team — yet he never made an effort to be part of the team.

Through the door, I hear a muffled command to come in. I purposefully came at the end of the lunch hour. Derek's receptionist has a propensity to be late and I fully took advantage to catch him off guard.

When I open the door, his expression is cartoon worthy. I wish I could use my Go Pro camera to catch the parade of emotions crossing his face. Unfortunately, Florida is a two-party state and I need Derek Zane's permission to record the conversation.

The thunderous expression on his face tells me this won't be a pleasant encounter. "Victoria Clarkson, did you forget you're no longer the ADA?" he asks snidely.

"No, actually I didn't forget. It's why I'm here," I declare as I stand my ground in the middle of his office.

Derek gestures dramatically toward the executive chairs. "Have a seat."

Gingerly, I sit on the edge of the chair and keep my back ramrod straight.

"Coffee?" He asks with a raised eyebrow.

"No thank you," I answer as politely as I can. "This isn't a social call."

"Oh great! I can't wait to hear what you have to say. I suppose you're going to sue us now. That's what people do who can't do their jobs."

"When?" I press.

"When, what?" he parrots.

"When exactly did you determine I couldn't do my job?"

Derek scowls at me as if I am the dumbest life form on the planet. "You know when! Have you been watching the news recently? They play that footage over and over again. It's as plain as day. If you're going to play with someone else's private parts, make sure there's not a camera around."

"You're right; I didn't know the building employee had a camera. But even if I did know, I wouldn't change anything I did that day. I helped save somebody's life. He was having such a severe anxiety attack, I was afraid he might have a stroke or a heart attack."

Derek smirks at me. "Oh, is that what we're calling it these days? It's all on tape. You can't dispute the tape," Derek argues.

"Actually, I can. The tape has been examined by a forensic expert with credentials issued by the FBI. The tape shows signs of being tampered with. It's been spliced together to show what you wanted to show. So, why?"

Derek breaks a pencil he was twirling between his fingers.

Undaunted by the power move I'd seen him pull countless times in court to impress the jury, I continue, "You can't argue I wasn't performing proper legal services for our office. We just had two huge profile wins which made you look spectacularly good."

He leans back in his big executive chair and loosens his tie. "I'm not responsible for how your sex tape was presented. Nobody's arguing you weren't a good assistant district attorney. Let's just say your unexpected altruism gave me all the cover I needed."

"Cover for what?"

"I suppose it wouldn't do me any good to tell you to leave this alone — because the whole time I've known you, you've never taken my advice about anything —"

"I know you don't believe this about me, but I am capable of making my own decisions," I assert, trying to hide my indignation.

Derek blows out a caustic burst of laughter. "Yeah, the view must be pretty good from the cheap seats. You have no idea what it's like to be in my position. It's impossible to make everyone happy in this job. There are voices in your ear all the time — crazy pressures from everywhere."

I stand up and face my former boss down. "So that's it? That's your official explanation. You threatened me with releasing the tape, but you aren't responsible for what's on the tape and you acknowledge that I'm a good ADA, but you let me go because there are pressures in your job. Did I get that right?"

"Geez, Clarkson. I forgot how good you are at drilling down an argument. Forget I said anything."

"No, I will not forget what you said. I'm not like my replacement."

It's all I can do not to laugh at the look of guilt on Derek's face.

"Oh, I've heard all about Ms. Hildabrand. Trust me, the reports I'm getting from inside and outside the legal system haven't been all that flattering. People have not been shy about sharing their opinions about my replacement."

Derek shakes his head and sighs. "I really wish you would've been more of a team player. If you had been, I could've done more to protect your job."

I draw myself up to my full height. "We have very different ideas about what it means to be a team player. In case you forgot, we took oaths to serve the people of Florida — not to promote our careers and make our friends and political cronies happy by doing the expedient thing."

Derek frowns at me as he heaves a deep sigh.

"Clarkson, you're a talented woman. Give yourself some time, you could land on your feet. I'm warning you. You don't want to open this can of worms. It could get ugly."

"Uglier than having my whole love-life debated on TV and my reputation dragged through the mud?" I counter with a raised eyebrow.

Derek points a finger in my face. "Don't say I didn't warn you. This isn't a fight you want to pick."

I shrug off his advice. "What are you going to do if I ignore your advice? Fire me?" With that parting remark, I turn on my heel and walk out of his office, feeling lighter than I have in months.

Chapter Thirteen

Cody

SLEEP IS A LUXURY these days. Between my caseload and stresses in my personal life, I'm beginning to wonder if I'll ever make friends with my bed again.

Just as I'm about to drift off, my cell phone beeps with the ring tone I've assigned to Toby Payne. I sit upright in bed as I grab my phone. My hands tremble as I unlock my phone and read the message. "Ready for a road trip? Isaac and the FBI are rounding up the team. Isadora is in Athens, Georgia. Rendezvous point is the parking lot of Identity Bank in two hours. No media notification."

Adrenaline makes me breathe quickly even though I'm only sitting on the bed when I text Toby, "10-4."

I place my phone on my nightstand and change back into my uniform and repack my go bag. I grab my phone and dial Tori's number. When she picks up the phone, the words I mentally rehearsed suddenly leave my brain and I stammer, "Hey, I'm sorry to call so late. The text came in from Toby."

The celebratory screech from the other end of the

phone is so loud, I have to hold the phone away from my ear.

"I guess you're awake now," I joke.

"Which one was found?" she asks, with breathless excitement.

"If I tell you, you have to keep it under your hat. This is not for public consumption yet," I caution

"Of course, that's a given."

"Everything indicates we found Isadora. I'm meeting with a team from the FBI. We're traveling to Georgia. That's why I called. I was hoping you might be able to watch Calico Jack while I'm out of town. I don't know how long I'll be gone, so I hate to use the boarding service."

"If it's all right with you, I'll stay at your house. I don't want Calico Jack to have to get used to a new environment," Tori suggests.

"That would be perfect. With his eyesight, sometimes he gets nervous when he goes to new places. I just bought groceries too. I'd hate for them to go to waste."

"Did Toby say if they were hopeful the other kids might be with her?"

"I don't know. We haven't had a chance to talk. One can always hope."

"I'll be right over. Let me pack an overnight bag and leave Bonni Jeanne a note."

"I hope you get here before I have to leave. We left things in a weird place and I'd like to see you before I go."

"I know, that felt strange to me too. I'll hurry, I promise."

Tori bursts through the front door with a duffel bag hanging off her shoulder and two large cups of coffee in her hands. "Sorry, I took a couple of minutes to go through the drive through. I figured you might appreciate it. You didn't say whether you were driving to Georgia or flying. A little caffeine never hurts either way. Although, it always sucks if you have to dump out your drink when you go through the security check," she rambles.

I take the coffee cups from her hands and place them on my sideboard and take a moment to search her expression. "Oh, Tor, I've missed you. Are we good?"

She smiles up at me and nods. "There was never a time when we weren't good. I just had to figure out where I was in my own head. So much has changed in my life recently, I had to find my bearings. It had nothing to do with defining 'us' really. Well, I guess it did — you scared me a little. Your declaration of support, as wonderful as it was, reminded me what I stood to lose if I didn't wake up and figure out what was important in my life."

I thread my arms around her waist and hold her loosely while we talk. "The last thing I wanted to do was scare you."

"I know you didn't. That was kind of the point. I've gotten good at holding people at arm's length while I pursued my career. Even when my life became chaotic and unmanageable with the crisis involving my mom, I forgot how to reach out and ask for help. I figured I could handle it all on my own. That kind of attitude eventually meant that when things snowballed out of control at work, I was all by myself."

"Well, not exactly. You have lots of supporters," I argue.

"I know that … now. But, part of the reason I know it is because you helped find those people who lined up in my corner. Otherwise, I would've still been shadowboxing with my enemies and nightmares, feeling isolated and alone."

For the first time in a few days, I feel hopeful again. "You don't feel that way now?" I venture tentatively.

"No," she answers. "Now I feel like I have a team behind me. I'm feeling like my old self — invincible and strong."

She stands up on her tiptoes and kisses me thoroughly. I'm so lost in the passion of the kiss, I almost miss her last words. "Thanks to you, I have a plan. I'll tell you all about it when you get back. Have a good trip, I'll keep the home fires burning."

I have to draw in a deep breath to steady myself. "Something tells me those home fires won't be as hot as my memories of this moment right here. I'm glad we could work out our timing issues this time, Tori."

An alarm goes off on my phone. "Crap. I could spend all night telling you how much you mean to me, but I gotta go."

"Go find those kids. You know where I'll be when you get back," Tori says as she gives me one last kiss and hugs me tight.

When I pull into the parking lot at Identity Bank, Isaac

greets me and knocks on my car window. "Hey, what took you so long? You aren't generally the last person to arrive." He steps aside to allow me to get out of my car. After I walk to the back of the car to get my bags, he takes the flashlight on his phone and looks closer at my face. "Oh, I see. You were otherwise occupied. Lucky for you Tristan's pilot decided to do a second maintenance check. If he hadn't, you might have missed the plane completely."

Reflexively, I wipe my lips with my thumb. Much to my chagrin, there is a smear of Tori's lipstick. "Why are we flying? Wouldn't it be just as fast to drive?"

Isaac throws his head back and laughs. "Obviously, you don't know my son-in-law very well. If he can take his private plane out for a spin, you know he will. Besides, flying there only takes about an hour and ten minutes. If we drove, it would take almost six hours by the time we stopped for breaks and gas."

"I've been on his private jet several times. I won't knock it," Toby adds.

As we stack the luggage in the back of Tristan's SUV, I turn back toward Toby. "Will you be okay with this? It'll probably hit close to home."

"I guess we'll find out," he responds with a shoulder roll meant to look casual — but under the dim glow cast by the dome light, I can see the tension in his body.

"You sure that's a good plan?"

"I'm not as green as I sound. I've been helping Jameson and Kendall on rescues. It's just that this is the first time I've done it face-to-face. Usually, I am behind-the-scenes, on the computer. It's like first mission jitters. I'm good."

"Okay, but if you need to bail, let me know. I understand. No judgment here. I know my first few missions after I was shot were a little shaky."

"Thanks, I appreciate knowing you got my back in more ways than one."

Toby and I wait in our nondescript uniforms as the tactical team moves out of sight of the door. Toby's hands shake a little as he holds the clipboard. I knock on the door. There is no answer, so I announce, "We're here to fix your Internet access."

After several seconds of complete silence, I gingerly open the door. My hand is on my weapon as I enter the cramped studio apartment. The stench of cigarette smoke is overwhelming.

My attention is captured by the woman curled up in a fetal position at the head of the bed. She appears to be clutching something in her hand. I have a split second to determine whether it's a gun. At that moment, Toby announces in an urgent tone, "Careful, there are kids here."

My gaze flicks over to him and I follow his line of sight down to the floor. Sure enough, there are two sets of feet peeking out from under the bed.

"Don't shoot!" The woman says as she flips her hair back away from her face. It is then I realize she is not a woman at all. She is a young girl — probably a teenager. "Please don't hurt us."

"Are you Isadora?" I ask, as I pull the reference picture out of my pocket and compare it to her. It is difficult to match this timid, disheveled and emaciated teenager to the bright, active athlete from the photograph.

"Why are you here?" she asks in a voice barely above a whisper.

"Are you alone?" I ask as I clear the rooms.

She holds stock still. "Who are you? Why do you want to know?"

Tristan squats down so he's eye to eye with Isadora. "I know you're scared. We're here to help you."

"For real?" she breathes.

I nod and flash my badge.

"Oh thank God! Hurry! He just went out for smokes. He'll be back."

"Anyone else here?" I ask.

"Just the kids." She looks toward the floor. "It's safe now, you can come out. These guys are the good guys."

As the kids are scrambling out from under the bed, I ask, "Any weapons?"

She tosses down the remote control, revealing her wrists under her long-sleeved shirt. It's then I notice she's handcuffed to the headboard with a bicycle chain. "Get real! If I had a weapon, do you think I would be stuck like this?"

Toby motions for me to toss him my handcuff keys.

He gently removes them and Isadora leaps into his arms. The kids literally scramble up my legs like tiny kittens.

I radio to the team outside and place a child on each hip and turn around and ask Isadora, "Do they have any medicine or anything they'll need in the next few hours?"

Isadora grabs a tattered blanket. "Only this." She holds it up for the kids to see. "See, Bobby, I didn't forget it."

"What about my doll?" the little girl asks.

"I'm sorry, Hannah. I can't get your doll back. But maybe we'll find another one that needs a family."

Toby shepherds everyone out the door. "I'm sorry, you said time was an issue. I'm trying to avoid a confrontation if we can."

Isadora shudders as she runs toward the door. "Wait, let Officer Erickson go first. Then you, then me," Toby instructs. He looks to me for confirmation.

"Mr. Payne is correct. There is a white van that looks like a cable van, but that is ours."

"What about car seats for the kids?" she asks as we hustle to the van.

Toby hops into the van first and puts his hand over Isadora's head to shelter it as he helps her step into the van. He sits down and holds his hand out to take the smallest child from me. He places the toddler in the seat next to him and buckles him in, carefully tightening the belt.

I place the older child in the next row back and buckle her in. I notice tears in her eyes. "It's okay, sweetie. We will get you somewhere safe."

"I'm hungry," she whispers as she sticks her thumb in her mouth.

"I'm sure we can get you something to eat after we get out of here," I answer.

Isadora's eyes dart around the van. "Will they be

okay? They've never gone anywhere with only seatbelts."

"We weren't expecting children, but we'll take care of that as soon as we get you out of immediate danger," I assured her as a voice comes over the radio advising me there are cars approaching.

Isadora hears the incoming chatter and her eyes widen. "I feel so dumb. We need to go. My *abuela* tells me nobody had car seats back in her day. They'll survive. I don't know what I was thinking."

"Let's go," I instruct the agent driving the car. "Get us to the closest law enforcement agency."

The agent quietly leaves the parking lot, driving slowly until we get to the thoroughfare. He speeds up when we join the flow of traffic.

He changes lanes and Isadora lets out a startled shriek and puts her arm across the toddler.

"I'm sorry, I'm being stupid," she mumbles under her breath.

Toby turns to her with a sober expression. "Don't worry about it. Your nerves are a little on edge. You've been through a lot. What you're experiencing is pretty normal."

"How do you know what's normal in a situation like this? Have you ever been kidnapped?"

Toby blushes bright red. "Yeah, I have. I always forget not everybody on the planet knows my story because it often feels like everyone does. Yeah, I was kidnapped when I was twelve years old. I was held for almost five years. So, I know exactly what you're feeling and what it feels like to have none of the thoughts in your head makes sense. Don't worry, that feeling gets better as you hang out with normal people in your world and reestablish relationships."

"You make it sound so easy. Everyone will know what happened. They'll think I'm a freak. I didn't ask for this to happen. I didn't want to be raped —" Isadora insists, breaking down into tears.

"We know — so will everyone else who matters," I assure her. "I have to ask you a few basic questions to figure out where we are in this situation. First, who are the children?"

"I can only tell you what I was told. Bex Michaels says they're his."

"You know your kidnapper's name?" I ask, unable to hide my surprise.

I look back to gauge her reaction. She shrugs as she responds, "I 'borrowed' his wallet one time when Bobby had the flu. He allowed me to be loose so I could take Bobby to the toilet. Bex left his wallet in the bathroom after his shower. I thought his name was weird. It sounded like the guy from Poison. My mom likes that band."

"I 'member that. It was gross. My brother puked on me. My dad got mad. I thoughted he was going to hit Bobby. But he hit Izzy instead. He gave her a black eye," Hannah explains.

"Any idea where their mother is?" I ask.

"Mommy's in jail. She stoll'ed some money. I wish she didn't. She's nicer than my daddy."

"Your daddy can't be mean to you now," Isadora says as she leans forward and strokes Hannah's hair.

When we pull up to the station, and Hannah sees the squad cars, she starts to cry. "Am I gonna have to go to jail like my mom?"

"No, honey. We did nothing wrong. These are the good guys. They are here to help us. Remember when we prayed every night for someone to come rescue us? That's why we're here," Isadora assures the kids.

"Does that mean my daddy is going to jail?"

"I don't know yet," I answer. "It's still too early to tell. We have to do an investigation and figure out what happened."

"He's a bad man, but he's still my dad. I don't want my brother and me to be left all alone."

I unbuckle Hannah and hitch her up on my hip. "I understand you're scared. I'll do everything I can to make sure you and your brother are safe."

"Izzy too?" she asks as she sticks her thumb in her mouth and lays her head on my chest.

"We'll take care of Isadora too, I promise."

But even as Toby helps the young woman out of the car and carries the toddler in his arms, I wonder to myself how difficult it will be to keep my simple promise.

Chapter Fourteen

Tori

"Bonni Jeanne! Guess what?" I greet as I come through my front door and dump my workout gear in front of the coat closet.

She rushes around the corner and stops to examine my somewhat puffy cheekbone. "Oh good Lord, did you tick off another trainer?"

I reach up to touch my sore cheek. "Oh, this? No, I just zigged when I should've zagged. I actually had a fabulous workout. My new trainer was teaching me some self-defense moves. He said I have solid skills. David wants me to help him teach the class next term."

"Hmm, Okay … if you say so. Your face looks like you were on the losing side of things."

"I swear, I wasn't. But that wasn't even the best thing that happened today —"

"I should hope not," Bonni Jeanne teases.

"Before I went to work out, I stopped by the rehab center and had lunch with my mom. Her hip is doing much better and they have her up and walking with a walker. Her new medicine is making a world of difference. She and I had a conversation, and it was almost like old times. She remembered me and my job and was even talking about what life was like with Dad before he passed away. Not only that, she knew about what was going on in the world. I mean, I know things aren't perfect, but it was the most normal I've seen her in years. I didn't want to leave."

"I don't blame you. If I were you, I would've wanted to stay. It must've been like a dream you didn't want to wake up from."

"Exactly! I was afraid to blink. I was sure I simply imagined it all. The nurse told me she's had more days like that, but she also cautioned me against tiring my mom out. So reluctantly I left. Who knows which version of my mom I'll encounter the next time I go see her? Even so, it was beautiful to have the mom I remember back even just for a few minutes."

Bonni Jeanne hugs me tightly around the neck. "I'm so happy for you. I hope this change is a sign of things to come. Maybe they finally made a breakthrough in her medication." Bonni Jeanne pulls away and wipes away her tears.

I walk to the refrigerator and grab a sports drink. When I walk into the dining area, I notice Bonni Jeanne standing there with a pensive expression on her face. "What's wrong?"

"I hate to do this to you because you've had such a great day."

"Do what?"

She hands me a letter. "It looks awfully official. I had to sign for it earlier today. I don't know about you, but when I get mail like that, it's never good news."

I examine the letter closely. It's from the Bar Association. "That's weird. I'm sure I paid my dues on time."

"Like I said, nothing good comes from mail you have to sign for. I'll let you have some privacy."

Bonni Jeanne turns to leave. I grab her shoulder. "Please don't leave me alone to cope with this. I have a hunch you're right. I don't want to face this alone."

With shaking hands, I open the letter. Silently, I read it. My knees buckle as my mind processes the words in the formal document.

"What? What does it say?"

"How can I be investigated for something that didn't happen?" I ask. "Can they really take my law license for something I didn't do?"

"Oh, Tori, I'm so sorry. Isn't there something you can do?"

"Honestly, I have no idea. I've never been through anything like this before."

"Well, I guess it's time for you to put your sharp legal mind to work and figure out how to save your job."

"Wow! You sound like Cody. If he were here, that's exactly what he would tell me to do."

"He did tell me to take good care of you. Consider yourself cared for."

I try to project confidence in my linen suit as the receptionist escorts me back to Mark Littleson's well-appointed office. It's surprising how quickly I got used to not being in professional mode. His office feels foreign even though I used to spend hours every day in places like this.

When Mark sees me, the tall Native American attorney grins and stands up to shake my hand. Even though his striking good looks and size should be intimidating, he is open and friendly. "Tori! It's great to see you. Cody mentioned you might be around. I am so glad you guys are dating now. Shelby thought you guys would make a great couple."

"She did?" I stammer.

"My wife likes to play armchair matchmaker," Mark explains. "I'm thrilled to see Cody happy for a change. He hasn't stopped talking about you. He's worse than my teenage daughter," he jokes with a wide grin.

"I can't believe Cody even said anything. Aside from that one time at the Aidan O'Brien concert, I've barely met any of his friends."

"Maybe not formally, but you've known a lot of us a long time."

"I guess so. I hope Cody was right. He told me his friends would be willing to help me if I was strong enough to ask."

"He was right. That's the way we do things around here."

"So, here I am asking. Asking for what I'm not sure. Advice? Maybe… Help? … Maybe… But you might not be able to. It may put you in ethical hot water."

"Don't worry about that. It is up to me to figure out my ethical boundaries. Just tell me what you need."

"Before I explain, I need to know how much you know about my current situation —"

"Only what I hear in the news … and Cody's general instructions for us to completely ignore what we hear."

"I agree with my boyfriend, you should ignore practically all of what you hear because the news reports are horribly incomplete. They have to be because they don't really know what happened. They try to guess based on what's happened in other high-profile cases, but they weren't there, so they don't really know."

"All the better to smear your reputation, right?"

"I guess — but I don't see the point."

"Eventually, this'll all blow over. We went through some messy stuff with Shelby when some jerk went after Savannah."

I hand the letter over to Mark. "That's why I'm here. It doesn't look like it'll blow over anytime soon. Now, it's more than just gossip. It's affecting my livelihood. This is serious."

Mark takes a few moments to read the letter from the Bar Association. He lets out a low whistle between his teeth. "First of all, let me say I'm so sorry. You don't deserve this. I've known you long enough to know you did nothing unethical. I don't care what the tape purports to show — it's bogus."

"I know that and you know that — but will the investigators for the Bar Association know? What am I going to do? I can't afford to hire a huge legal team to fight this!"

"I say don't fight it. If you didn't do anything wrong, their investigation won't find any evidence against you. I don't represent clients in these kinds of situations, and I don't want to do you a disservice — but I will help you find someone who can represent you."

I frown at Mark. "Didn't you hear me? I've got no money to fight this. I haven't been working. I've been taking care of my mom and she has huge medical bills."

"Don't worry about that part. We'll figure it out later. I think this will be the break you need."

"I don't know. I hinted to my boss that I had already had a forensic evaluation done on the tape and that it showed it had been spliced. The weird thing is he didn't even seem surprised. He just said he had political pressure to get me out of my job."

"Derek Zane was always prettier than he was smart. I can't believe he admitted that to you. Did he happen to mention who he was receiving political pressure from?"

I shake my head. "He's dumb, but not quite that dumb. I have a few guesses though. I still have a few connections at my old office. Apparently, my new replacement is awfully cozy with Councilman Warren. He meets with her in her office several times a week."

"How often did you meet with council members when you worked there?"

"Next to never. The only time I ever saw them was at awkward fundraising events and at mandatory trainings for the county."

"Aside from the videotape, did you guys talk about anything else?"

"No not really. I just wanted to know why in the heck he fired me after I'd scored two major case victories for the District Attorney's Office. It's not like I was an embarrassment to the office or anything. I had done pretty well. I didn't hog all the credit like he usually does.

I thank my whole team — including him. So, I was pretty shocked when he came and told me he was firing me. I knew I had done absolutely nothing wrong."

I point to the letter Mark is still holding in his hands. "I guess my innocence doesn't really matter now because the bar is going to investigate me as if I'm a criminal. Do you know I was scared to take notes into an open note exam during law school because I was afraid it was somehow cheating even when I was given permission to do so? That's the kind of person I am. I'd never do anything to jeopardize a case!" I practically yell into Mark's face.

"Tori, I know this about you. As soon as the investigators talk to you and get your side of the story and look at that ridiculous videotape, they'll know it too."

I take a few breaths and try to compose myself. I know Mark is not the enemy. Everyone I know who knows Mark Littleson knows he is a calm and reasonable person. Savannah, who has every reason on the planet to hate all men, thinks he is one of the finest people on the whole planet. I need to reel myself in and calm down. If I talk this way to anyone from the State Bar Association, I'm toast.

"Part of the reason I'm so upset is because someone I trusted to have my back in court was the one who turned me in. Isn't that the craziest thing ever? Like I'm not dealing with enough crap in my life right now!"

"I know it's frustrating. But here's the thing… An investigation by the Bar Association is a good thing. They have to appoint people who don't know you or any of the other witnesses in the case. It's somebody impartial. So, when they do an investigation and clear your name, you'll be able to go back to work without a stain on your reputation."

I flop back against the luxurious leather chair. "I know you're right. You're totally right. But it still makes me so mad. This should've never happened. Why wasn't my boss on my side if he values what I do?"

"Because Zane is a self-absorbed prick?"

I let out a surprised burst of laughter. "Oh right! I forgot you know my boss."

"I do. I had that opinion before you ever walked through my office door. Now, you've just cemented it."

"Still, I wish I had more solid evidence that I'm innocent. I didn't even know the building maintenance person had a camera. Heck, I don't even know their name. I wasn't even paying close enough attention to know whether it was a man or a woman. It could've been either. I know the person had a uniform on and a baseball cap. There was some sort of name tag sewn onto the uniform, but I didn't take the time to read it because I was focused on the witness. His demeanor was so disconcerting, he had all of my attention. He was a nervous wreck, and I was afraid he would have a heart attack right in front of me. I literally was thinking to myself I wonder if I remember enough CPR to help him until the ambulance arrives if something happens."

"Under those circumstances I can understand why you wouldn't notice the maintenance person."

"So, I don't see how there's any hope I could come up with any evidence because I don't know who took the video."

"This sounds like a job for Isaac or Tristan and Identity Bank. They are better at getting this sort of thing than I am. A good lawyer could probably get a court order for something like that from the news media, but it could take a while. Tristan tends to be able to sweet-talk his way through dilemmas like that."

"He is amazing. I've worked with him on a few cases but right now he's helping Cody out. They're looking for some missing teenagers. I hate to distract him from that. It's a much more urgent situation than what I've got going on."

"Identity Bank is huge. Isaac and Tristan are not the only people who work there. If they can't help you themselves, they've got other people who could get you what you need. Let me place a few calls for you, okay?"

"Okay, whatever you think is best because I'm more than just a little freaked out by this letter."

"Go ahead and respond to the letter. Answer the questions the best way you know how, and we'll do what we can to unearth more evidence to help you."

"I can't tell you how much I appreciate this. Cody was right. He does have the greatest friends on the planet."

Mark grins at me. "Thank you. We try."

CHAPTER FIFTEEN

CODY

WHEN I FINALLY MAKE it home, I'm exhausted to the bone. I'm a little puzzled when Calico Jack doesn't meet me at the door like he usually does — but a quick tour of my place quickly turns up the answer.

Tori is curled up in the middle of my bed with her computer in front of her. Calico Jack is sheltered in her arms. She's wearing my favorite pair of headphones and she's sound asleep. She doesn't even stir when Calico Jack realizes I'm in the room. He jumps off the bed and dances around my feet. He yips excitedly and begs for me to pick him up.

When I pick him up, he licks my face. I try to stifle my laugh at his silly antics. I set him on the bed and try to quietly grab blankets from the linen closet. Unfortunately, one of the blankets is stuck on a box of spare Christmas decorations and the whole thing crashes down.

Tori sits straight up in bed and screams. Calico Jack starts to growl at me. "Hey? What's that about? You were licking my face thirty-seconds ago. Oh, I see; you have to protect the damsel in distress now." It's then I notice Tori doesn't seem to be quite awake as she looks at me blankly. "Tori, wake up! It's only me," I urge as I walk over and gently shake her shoulder.

"I see that now!" she exclaims sardonically. "A hello would've worked just fine. Come to think of it, aren't handsome Prince Charming types like yourself supposed to wake someone like me up with a sweet kiss instead of a racket loud enough to wake the dead?"

I feel my face heat with embarrassment. "Honestly, I didn't intend to wake you up at all. You looked so beautiful and peaceful laying there I was planning to let you sleep. Obviously, I need to do a better job of housekeeping because I was trying to get some extra bedding when my closet exploded with Christmas decorations."

"Okay, that's plausible. Can we just have a do-over? I've been waiting for days for you to come home. This is not how I wanted to greet you. I'm really not this kind of person. I'm just stressed out and exhausted."

"Sounds good. Let's start over." I stand up and leave the bedroom. I turn around and stand in the hallway. I tentatively knock on the door frame as I announce. "I'm home."

Tori hops off the bed and sprints toward me. With a grin, I realize she's wearing one of my favorite baseball jerseys. It's one that Dylan got me when we were on an undercover operation. It has Mickey Mouse splashed across one side. Funny thing, it never looked nearly as great on me as it does on her, paired with a pair of tight yoga pants. It looks like it was made for her. I mean, it's just a goofy novelty shirt. On her, it's a designer dress.

Her hair is tied back with a folded bandanna and her

feet are bare with bright red toenails with, ironically, silver Mickey Mouse silhouettes. She catches me looking at them and flexes her toes. "Aren't these perfect?"

"There isn't anything about you that's not perfect."

She puts a hand up toward her hair and says, "You're such a liar. My hair is a rat's nest and my clothes look like pajamas."

I tilt my head to scrutinize her. "Okay, your clothes might look a little like pajamas, but at least they're cute pajamas."

"Just as I thought, there's no excuse for my hair," she retorts, before I can say anything.

I grab her hands and pull her close. I capture her lips in a lingering kiss many days in the making. "Oh, man. There aren't enough words to tell you how much I've missed you. Let me tell you, there isn't a single thing wrong with your hair. It looks soft and wild. Exactly the way I like it. I can't stand women who shellac their hair with product."

"Guys do it too," she argues defensively.

"Not this guy. Besides, have you ever tried to touch that stuff? It's gross."

Tori runs her hand through my short cropped hair. "Obviously, you don't need it. Your hair is perfect. Just like the rest of you." She stands up on her tiptoes and kisses me again.

I pull away and fish something out of my pocket. "Close your eyes."

"Should I be scared?"

"I don't think so," I answer, trying to cover my nerves. It's been a long time since I've cared about a woman enough to put my heart on the line like this.

Much to my relief, Tori dutifully closes her eyes.

"Hold out your wrist please." Tori looks like she's having difficulty complying with my simple request.

"Do you trust me?" I ask, teasingly. But I hold my breath for her answer.

She nods. "I do, but it's hard."

I flinch even though I try not to.

"Don't take it personally. I'm having a hard time trusting anybody these days."

"Maybe you can trust yourself," I say as I fasten a three toned bracelet on her wrist. Each strand has a different word engraved on it. The first band says believe, the second says strength, and the third says justice.

Her eyes pop open when she feels the cool metal against her wrist. She gasps when she sees the delicate bracelet. "Oh my gosh, this is beautiful." She examines it closer and sees the words. She takes a shallow breath. "It's perfect!"

"Happy birthday, Tori. I'm sorry I had to be gone."

Tears leak from the corners of her eyes. "I didn't even know you knew it was my birthday. I understand why you had to go."

"Birthdays are kinda my thing. I've known about yours for a while. The timing just sucked for you but coming home to you was the best present I could hope for and it's not even my birthday."

Tori holds up her wrist and jingles the little metal bangles in her bracelet. "I don't know. I think I did okay. This bracelet is perfect for me. Some days, I get discouraged and forget what's important. This will be the perfect reminder for me to focus on what's important. Thank you so much. I love it." She stands on her tiptoes and kisses me. "Now, tell me why I'm the best thing about your day. What happened while you were gone?"

I heave a huge sigh as I place my arm around her waist and escort her back over to the bed. I stack a bunch of pillows against the headboard and pat the spot next to me. She curls up beside me and makes a spot for Calico Jack. After we're all comfortable, I sort through my thoughts and decide what I can tell her. A lot of it has already been leaked to the newspaper so technically, it's public information — much to my captain's dismay.

"Well, let's just put it this way. Nothing unfolded quite like we expected it to. We found Isadora, but she wasn't alone."

Tori jerks upright and stares at me with wide-eyed amazement. "You found all the missing teens?"

I shake my head regretfully. "I wish that were true. Unfortunately, that's not what we found. Isadora's kidnapper had two of his own children — or so it seems. The oor kids aren't even old enough to go to school yet."

"Where's their mom?"

"Would you believe this? Felena Hopner was already in jail awaiting trial for fraud and identity theft. So, for all intents and purposes, those kids are orphans."

"That's sad," Tori says as she snuggles closer to my chest.

"Oh, you haven't seen sad. They were so bonded to Isadora, they didn't want to leave her side, even when their aunt came to get them. They begged to stay with Isadora. It broke her heart. She should have been happy to reunite with her own family, but she was so distraught over the kids' reaction, she couldn't be happy for her own reunification. It was a giant mess."

"How devastating for her! I can't even imagine. Is she getting counseling? I imagine it's damaging for her. Those kids were like her family."

"That's all covered. Whatever her insurance doesn't cover, Tristan has an anonymous benefactor who works with the charity, Locate My Heart, to grant money to families who need help after someone has gone missing."

"Oh, that's very generous."

"Yeah, so she'll have all the counseling resources she needs."

"I hate to ask this, but does she know what happened to the other kids like Dashonte's brother?"

"We're working to figure that out. I guess occasionally, there were other kids who came through. They didn't stay long. Isadora said Bex was sort of like a clearing house for the other kids. He kept them separate from her and his own kids. The only time Isadora had any interaction with the other kids was way back at the beginning of her captivity. Apparently, Isadora is a dead ringer for Bex's wife, and the kids behaved better for her, so he kept her around instead of auctioning her off to the highest bidders like he did the others."

I feel a shudder go up Tori's spine. "That is one of the creepiest things I've ever heard. I guess it turned out to be a break for Isadora because at least you were able to locate her."

"Jameson and the rest of Tristan's team at Identity Bank are working on it around-the-clock. Additionally, Jameson has recruited his wife Kendall and her organization, Locate My Heart, which specializes in searching for missing children.”

“Oh, that’s right, they helped to track down, Toby Payne, correct?”

“Yeah, that’s how Jameson and Kendall met.”

“How does your boss feel about all the civilian help? I know agencies can be territorial.”

“Look, at this point these kids have been missing for so long, we’re treating this like one big task force. The more the merrier at this point. We need as many resources as we can get. Every day they’re missing puts them in more danger. The more time I spend with Toby Payne, the more that’s drilled into me. I figured I knew all about missing children. I studied it at the academy, I’ve even gone to special workshops held by the FBI and the National Missing and Exploited Children organization. I thought I was pretty cognizant of the dangers and the way the perpetrators operated. In reality, I knew nothing.”

Tori strokes her hand down my face. “You can’t beat yourself up. I felt the same way after we spent that night with him putting the information into the computer. I put the bad guys on trial all the time but it’s a whole different experience hearing the whole story from the mouth of the victim without the pressure of a formal interview and the veneer of law enforcement roles between us. Hearing Toby honestly tell us how it impacted his life will forever change my life.”

“I don’t know about you, but I don’t sleep the same now. His words penetrate my dreams.”

“I thought I was thorough when I prosecuted child sex predators before, but if I ever get to practice law again, Lord help the next one. I will be so much more prepared. They won’t know what hit them.”

I shift in my position to look at her. "What do you mean *if* you ever get to practice law? Why can't you simply find another prosecutor position in another county?"

Tori hangs her head. "I didn't want to tell you this while you were gone because I didn't want to add to your stress level."

I lift her chin with my finger. "You can never be just another stressor in my life. You mean too much to me."

"Zane is trying to have me disbarred."

"What? Is he bonkers? It's one thing to play games with office politics. It's another thing to mess with someone's livelihood. Is he absolutely insane? I can have a 'discussion' with him. I don't mean the rational kind either."

Tori shakes her head. "The Bar has to do its process. I have no idea what he's thinking, or what the outcome might be. I can guess, but I might be wrong. After all, the whole eastern seaboard knows about what I allegedly did in that stupid elevator."

"The key word is allegedly. You didn't do squat!"

"Yeah, I know that, and you know that … but the only people who know what really happened are Mr. Cavanaugh and whoever the building maintenance person was. But I don't think I'm allowed to talk to them and, because you're my boyfriend, I doubt if you're allowed to talk them either."

"Please tell me you have a lawyer," I plead as I watch her bottom lip tremble.

"Not yet. I tried to tell Mark I have no money to hire one. Unfortunately, Mark doesn't handle cases like this. He said he would hire me the most qualified attorney he could."

"Well yeah," I answer somewhat sarcastically. "Of course he should. This is your freaking career we're talking about here — one you happen to be awesome at. You shouldn't lose your law license for something you didn't do. That's the most idiotic thing I've ever heard."

"Mark tells me an investigation by the Bar Association is probably the best thing that could happen because it will help clear my name. I'm hoping he's right, but you know it was a sucky thing to happen — especially on my birthday."

"I can tell you one thing, aside from you, Mark is one of the smartest people I know. If he tells you this is a positive development, you can take it to the bank."

"Are you sure? I'm afraid to put my faith in any good news recently."

I point to her bracelet. "Yeah, I'm sure. You have the facts on your side. Not only that, you've got a great reputation and a solid record behind you. I don't know how all the planets lined up to cause you to lose your job, but I have a feeling it actually had very little to do with you. When all the facts come out, I think you'll be vindicated and a lot of injustices will be exposed."

Tori runs her fingers over the metal bangles. "My life is so scary right now. I feel like I'm teetering between love and injustice. It could go so right or so wrong in the blink of an eye."

"Just so you know, I'm clearly rooting for love," I respond as I gather her in my arms and hold her tight.

Chapter Sixteen

Tori

I PAUSE BEFORE I go through the doors of Ink'd Deep. I can't believe I'm about to do this. I used to be straight-laced and all about projecting the proper image — but suddenly, all that doesn't seem quite so important anymore. The me who I thought it was disappeared several months ago along with my mother's memories of me. Having to fight for my right to my professional identity and a spot in my mother's ever more rattled brain woke me up and helped me set some priorities. Being true to myself became one of them.

When I open the door to the tattoo parlor, a chorus of people greet me by name. Reflexively, my jaw drops and I look behind me to see if they're talking to someone else named Tori.

Jade, one of the owners of Ink'd Deep, greets me, "Hey, Beautiful, what can I do for you today?"

"Are you sure you're talking to me?" I ask as I look down at one of Cody's old baseball jerseys and my yoga pants. Somehow it's become my favorite go-to uniform.

The corner of Jade's mouth hitches up. She looks

over at a rough biker type guy lying face down on a bench getting a back piece. "I like Skeeter and all, but I'm not sure I'd call him beautiful. Even if I did, his woman might have something to say about it."

The guy snickers, "Yeah, she'd tell you to go have your eyes checked."

Jade glances back at me. "So, I guess I mean you —
"

"Oh, okay. Well —" I stammer awkwardly, "are you busy?"

Jade grins. "As a matter of fact, I'm not. My afternoon appointment canceled because she had to take her kid to the orthodontist. Something about snapped bands or something. It all sounded very painful. So, what do you need? I'm up for a challenge today."

"I guess that's good. I suppose you've heard what's going on with me?" I let my speech trail off. I'm so tired of having to explain it to everyone.

"Let's say the rumor mill hasn't been kind to you. We get lots of law enforcement types in here," Jade responds with a grimace.

My stomach drops to my toes. "So, am I winning or losing in the court of public opinion?"

"With the loudmouth jerks? Losing. With the people whose opinion I respect? Overwhelmingly winning."

My eyebrows raise in surprise. "Well, I guess that's something. I wish it was as simple as winning over the public. Now, they're after my law license. I don't know if you've heard about that lovely development. That's why I'm here. I can't sit and wait anymore."

"I can't imagine. If I were in your shoes, I would be

riding my motorcycle everywhere," Jade commiserates.

"It was one thing when I was at home taking care of my mom. She took up a lot of my time. I can only work out so much. My body can't take any more stress. If I'm not careful, I'll permanently injure myself. I can't stand to watch the news because I can't do much to change it. I still have to act as if I might get my job back so I can't become overtly politically active because I might go back to my position. I can't go look for another job because I don't even know if I'll still be a licensed attorney."

"How frustrating for you! How can I help?" Jade asks.

"The other night as I was waiting for Cody to come home from work, I got to thinking about losing everything. I worked exceptionally hard to graduate in the top of my class. I got a lifetime of learning invested in my career as a prosecutor. Somehow I want to acknowledge and recognize everything that I've put in to becoming the person I am. I don't know if I'm going to win or lose this fight with the bar and the guy who is out to get me. But somehow I want to honor the person I am — or at least who I was before I was wrongfully terminated. Deep down inside, even if they take away the number which allows me to practice law, I'm still a fierce fighter and advocate who wants to make the world better. So, I want to get a tattoo to show that. It's not for anybody else it's just for me."

Jade puts down her sketchpad and silently walks over and puts her arms around me. "It's okay. I believe you. I believe other people will believe you too. Even if they don't, it doesn't change who you are on the inside," she murmurs softly against my temple.

For a long time we simply stand there and I absorb

her strength. After a while, I take a shaky breath and whisper, "Thank you, you have no idea how much I needed that."

"I don't exactly, but I've been in a situation where my whole life was turned upside down and I lost my sense of identity. It took the love of another person for me to find myself."

"It's funny you should say that. I told Cody the other day that it felt like I was stuck between love and injustice and I didn't know which way the scales would tip."

"That's actually a great idea for a tattoo. How do you feel about Lady Justice?"

"I love *Iustitia*. We had this huge statue in my law library. Whenever I felt discouraged or too tired to study, I would look up at it and remind myself why I was there. She gave me courage to push through and study harder. I went to law school to make a difference in the world. All these years later, I still feel the same passion."

"Okay, give me a few minutes to draw something up. Where do you want this bad boy?"

"I'm often accused of wearing my heart on my sleeve. Let's make that literal. I've got nothing to hide. I'm going to have some fun pointing that out to some people in my life who can't seem to get a clue."

Jade gives me a small salute as she picks up a handful of pencils and heads back to her light board. "It's a plan. I love it when my tattoos can carry a message. This will be fun. Welcome to Ink'd Deep. I'm so happy you came in today."

Cody looks absolutely wrecked when he comes in my back door after work. He walks over to hug me and I back out of his arms. A blank look crosses his face and he tries to disguise his hurt. I place my hand on his forearm as he turns to leave. "Wait, don't go. I'm just a little sore," I confess as I pull up the sleeve of the baseball jersey.

When he sees Jade's artwork under the clear plastic, he whistles softly. "Gotta admit, I'm more than a little jealous. I've wanted Jade to scribble on me for a while. How did you talk her into it?"

I shrug. "I got lucky, I guess. I just asked."

"Maybe I'm not as charming as you are. She's always busy when I try to book an appointment. You know, she's booked out like two years?"

"Really? She never said a word. One of her clients had a dental emergency."

"Jade must adore you. She has a wait list a mile and a half long. How ever you got your piece, it is gorgeous. We should go out and celebrate. I'm feeling stir crazy. Does Jade care if you go outside with that?"

"I'm sure she doesn't want me to go sunbathing. As long as I keep it covered, I'm sure it's fine."

"I feel like going to the beach. There is this awesome little crab shack that sets up shop near Crescent Beach."

I can't hide my surprise. "I guess it's a good thing I ate a snack. That's a long way from home."

"Don't worry, I'm a good driver. I took defensive driving," Cody jokes as he grabs one of my jackets from the coat closet.

"What about Calico Jack?" I ask.

"He's already out in your side yard waiting for us."

"Oh, I guess you were pretty certain I'd say yes?" I tease as I bump his hip on the way past him. I grab a bag of dog treats I was planning to take over to Cody's house.

Cody sees me out of the corner of his eye. "Hey! No wonder Calico Jack likes you best. Do you do that all the time?"

I nod. "Of course. Don't worry, he's not the only one I spoil. Why do you think I make you chocolate chip cookies every week?"

"You don't always make me chocolate chip cookies. Sometimes you make me peanut butter cookies," Cody argues sarcastically.

I shrug. "What can I say? I like to keep the men in my life happy."

"You do make me incredibly happy. Calico Jack too, it seems," he says as he eyes the treats glumly.

I pat him on the top of the head. "Poor baby! You didn't tell me we were going to go anywhere, so I didn't have a goodie bag packed for you. Give me a minute and I can get one."

Cody grins like a seven-year-old kid. "You are the absolute best! Do whatever you have to do. I'll go round up Calico Jack and get him ready to go."

I stand on my tiptoes and kiss Cody on the cheek as I hand him the bag of dog treats. "You may need these. I'll have your treats later."

My face heats as Cody winks at me and murmurs, "Promises, promises, promises —"

Cody pops the last bite of crab in my mouth. I close my eyes and savor the last buttery bite. It is all I can do not to moan. "Okay, I can't believe I've missed out on this my whole life."

"What do you mean?" Cody asks as he laughs at my expression. "Haven't you had fresh crab before?"

"Probably not this fresh," I admit. "I've never eaten at a place like this. Growing up, my mom was a real stickler for cleanliness. In her mind, that meant eating only at establishments with tablecloths and cloth napkins — of course, that ruled out any place like this."

"That's too bad. That's one of my favorite perks about being a cop. I get to go into people's neighborhoods and find out the best places to eat. Some of them look pretty shady, but the locals know where the best food is. I've traveled to a lot of different places — especially working undercover — sometimes, the food is the best part. Contrary to what people believe, I don't always eat donuts and coffee, although Dylan and I have consumed more than our fair share of those too."

I take a moment to ogle his body, pausing for a second to appreciate his ridiculous abs. "You keep saying that, but I find it hard to believe. You and Palmer are in remarkably good shape. You guys can't eat as much junk food as you say you do."

Cody throws his head back and laughs. "We do! It's only because Palmer busts my butt at the gym too."

"How is he? It had to be a big blow not to find Tallulah Johnson when you guys located Isadora."

Cody puts his elbows on the picnic table and rubs his temples. "It was hard on all of us. We want to solve every case as quickly as possible. When we didn't find all the missing kids together, it was like a roundhouse kick to the jaw. Even worse, when Isadora found out there were three other kids her age who were still missing, she was destroyed. She saw other kids, but she didn't realize they had also been kidnapped. She thought they might've been involved with drug deals or something. She had no idea they suffered the same fate she did. She's worn herself out trying to remember every single conversation she had with Bex Michaels. She's even trying hypnosis."

"Oh my gosh, poor baby. She needs to be moving on with her life — not trying to relive every second of her captivity. How awful for her."

"I feel the same way. But on the other hand, everything she can give us is helpful. I want to protect her. Fortunately, the agent in charge is being exceptionally careful and working with her psychologist so I feel better about it — but it's still not an ideal situation. I've heard any suggestion to her to slow down and take it easy is being met with huge resistance. She wants to nail these guys and find the rest of the kids. She is driven and focused."

"I can't imagine. Her whole life is forever changed by this."

"I know. I guess Toby Payne has kept in touch with her and is helping her with her transition back into the real world."

"That is sweet of him. This can't be easy for him either."

"I can't imagine it is. But I think helping other people

is a good thing for him. He spent a lot of years being the victim. Being a hero is a good fit for him."

"Speaking of being a hero, how are you? You spent a lot of time asking me how I was doing when you were out of town, but you didn't talk much about how you're coping with all this."

"Well, I'm alive … and I should probably buy stock in the company who makes Tums and No-Doze. I worry a lot these days. I worry we won't get to the other kids in time, I worry about the damage being done to them while we scramble to find them, I worry about the damage already done to Isadora, I worry about the kids I didn't even know existed before we found her. I worry about the nameless, faceless strangers who take these kids. Will we be able to find enough evidence to nail their balls to the wall?"

"That's a lot of worrying —"

"Oh, that's not even the half of it —"

"When do you find time to sleep?"

"I don't. That's part of the problem. That's why we're wandering around the beach eating crab legs from a mobile crab shack. I finally reached my limit. I've hit a wall where I can't take any more. Reports are bleeding together and I can't tell one Internet site from another. My soul desperately needs recharging, so I'm stepping back and playing hooky at the beach with you. I just can't cope anymore."

I pull Cody up to a standing position and wrap my arms around his waist. As I rest my head on his chest and listen to the steady beat of his heart, the role reversal is not lost on me. "How hard is it for you to take care of yourself for a change?"

Cody glances down at me and the corner of his mouth hitches up. "Am I really that transparent?"

"I don't get to take care of you often. Usually you're the one fixing me up after life beats me up. This is nice. I could get used to holding you and kissing your boo-boos."

Cody reaches up and points to his bottom lip. "I think I'm a little sore right here Ms. Clarkson."

Grinning, I stand on my tiptoes and kiss him lightly. "There, is that better?"

He scoops me up in his arms and takes his time as he explores my mouth with a sensual kiss. Just as I relax against his chest, his phone rings. It's the theme song from Magnum PI.

"Crap! That's Dylan. He knew I was on a date with you. If he's interrupting, it's important."

I wiggle in his arms and try to reach his phone. "Answer it! If anybody understands how our jobs don't fit into convenient hours, it's me."

Cody reluctantly puts me down and digs through his jacket pocket which he left on the picnic bench. "If Palmer doesn't have a life and death emergency, he's gonna buy lunch for the next two months," he grumbles under his breath. His phone stops ringing before he can get to it, but Palmer immediately calls back.

When Cody answers the phone, he says "This better be important — you know what I had planned —"

I can't hear what Dylan Palmer says, but whatever it is, it sounds strident.

Cody looks like he's been hit by a two by four.

"No sh —" He looks up at me with wide eyes.

"Where is he now? I'll meet him back at the station in two hours. If he only wants to talk to me, tell the captain to respect his wishes. His family doesn't trust the police very much. I don't want to freak him out. Is Dashonte with him?"

As Cody listens to Palmer on the phone, I collect our belongings and stuff them into my oversized tote bag. After Cody hangs up, I try to contain my curiosity. I realize I'm not fully involved in the case even though technically I'm a paid assistant. I'm dying to know what's going on, but I don't want to jeopardize the case. So, I walk quietly beside Cody for a few minutes before I finally asked, "Does that mean what I think it means?"

"I'm not exactly sure what it means yet. DeAndre just walked into the precinct to report his own kidnapping — but the only detective he wants to speak with is me."

"Any reason why?"

"Not a clue. I guess we'll find out in a couple of hours."

"You were part of Isadora's rescue, is it possible he knows?"

"Isadora swears she doesn't know any of the other kidnapping victims, so on the surface, that doesn't seem likely — but I guess you never know in cases like this. We'll have to see how it all plays out."

As we get back to Cody's car, he opens a safe in a hidden compartment in his trunk. He pulls out a laptop and tosses me the keys. "Do you mind driving? I have to review case notes before I talk to DeAndre."

I smile. "No problem. I'm always happy to play chauffeur when I get to drive your hot rod. I won't get a speeding ticket because the car belongs to a law enforcement officer, right?" I add with a wink.

Cody swallows hard. "Nah, that's pure urban legend. You have to treat my baby much more gently — otherwise terrible things happen to her insides."

I grin mischievously. "Don't worry. Responsible is my middle name."

Chapter Seventeen

Cody

WHEN I ENTER THE interrogation room, DeAndre gives me a sullen scowl. "Took you long enough."

I have to cover my shock when I see the gaunt teenager with swollen black eyes. If it were not for his defiant body language and the slight Jamaican accent in his voice, I'd swear I was looking at a different kid. Finally, I find my voice and respond to his criticism, "Sorry, I was out of town. Got here as quickly as I could."

"My brother said I could trust you," he blurts. "Is he right? You're not just BS-ing me and making me wait because you like to see me suffer?"

"No, I wouldn't lie to you. I was up at Crescent Beach. I can show you my receipt for the crab shack."

"Okay, I get it. It's just that I don't trust anybody these days. People suck."

"I don't blame you. If I were in your shoes, I'd feel the same way."

"What did Dashonte tell you about what happened?" DeAndre asks.

"He didn't know. He was just worried because no one

could find you."

"Yeah, I bet everybody assumed I took off with gang bangers again."

"It was something we investigated, sure. But all the evidence pointed to the fact you've been turning your life around," I insist.

DeAndre smirks. "I thought I was and then apparently the cockroaches from our apartment ate my brain."

"What do you mean?" I ask, surprised by his odd statement.

"Well, my mom and my parole officer were telling me to be careful about who I hang with. So, I've been paying attention to my peeps, or at least I thought it was. So, I've been minding my business and learning to skateboard. I've been watching vintage Tony Hawk videos and a bunch of stuff online. I was practicing my skills and getting pretty dope."

"That's cool."

"When I started hanging out with a bunch of new people at the new skate park, I even had my PO run their names to make sure they were straight with the law because you know I didn't want to mess with any low lives and start that all sh — stuff over again —"

"Smart strategy," I mumble as I continue to take notes.

"I thought so too. We had a tight group and things were going great for a few months. So, then this new guy started coming around. Ig said he was documenting stuff for his YouTube channel. He had business cards and everything. I started following his channel. He had lotsa different channels. One was for extreme sports. He had another one for artists. He had another one for musicians — it was kinda cool. He had like this whole thing for underground artists and creative types. It was like the anti-cool kid thing. I knew some people from my school and from some other schools around the area. Lots of people posted on his YouTube channels. It seemed totally legit — even some of the kids' parents were posting comments."

"Did this Ig guy ever ask to film you?"

"No, not at first. In the beginning, he was filming the architecture of the park. Then, he was filming the graffiti for his art channel. Ig asked one of my friends if he could film some of his moves for his extreme sports channel. My friend said, 'Sure.' Pretty soon, the footage was up on the Internet and he made like this cool music video out of it. The video was like something you would see on ESPN — it was totally rad. The next time, Ig asked me if I would throw down a few moves and I said, 'Okay, just edit it out if I fall down'. He laughed like it was some huge joke and a couple weeks later, my video was up on his YouTube channel. It made me a huge hit with my friends at school. It was like I was popular, like a rap star or something."

"I bet that was a fun experience."

"Yeah, most people from my neighborhood don't get noticed for much at school except when we get in trouble. My PE teacher even played it for our class."

"So, what happened next?"

"The next time I talked to him, Ig said my video was one of the most popular he ever posted on his site. He wanted to know if I wanted to have my own channel. Of course, I was blown away. I always wanted to be an X

Gamer, but I knew I could never get sponsors on my own, but if I had a YouTube channel, maybe someone would notice me. He told me it takes money to film all the stuff and he would have to meet with some investors down in Jacksonville."

"Did he want you to meet with these investors too?"

DeAndre nods. "Yeah, that's where I should've gotten a clue. He told me the only time that these investors could meet with me was during class. I lied to my mama and skipped school. I did all the stuff I knew not to do. I got in the car with somebody I didn't know — heck, I still don't know his real name. He just went by Ig. I didn't know where we were headed, who we were meeting, and I didn't tell anybody where we were going. Ma is going to kill me."

"I'm sure your mom is just grateful to have you back in one piece. Everybody makes mistakes. It doesn't matter how old you are. That's what makes predators so dangerous. They don't present all this stuff up front with danger signs. They drip little pieces of information a tiny bit at a time so it doesn't seem like a big deal. Of course, when you look back on it you can see all the mistakes you made — but when you were making them, they didn't seem like dangerous moves."

DeAndre hangs his head. "Dashonte told me I had to tell you this to help catch the bad guys. I need to go to the hospital."

"Okay," I reply, shifting gears in my head as a knot forms in my stomach. "Do you want Dashonte to go with you?"

"Oh heck no! I don't need my brother there while they're examining my private parts. You know, I learned about this crap in my health class. I just never thought it would happen to me. I thought rape was a girl problem."

"Sadly, it's not. People think it is, but the truth is one in six boys are sexually assaulted in their lifetime. The real number is probably even higher. You're not alone."

"The investor guy said because I had sex with him, it means I'm gay now. Was he right?"

"No! Let me tell you what it means. It means he's a criminal. He's a pedophile, rapist, and a kidnapper. He's a liar, a psychopath, and a creep. You can't turn a heterosexual person gay any more than you can turn a gay person straight. It doesn't work that way," I assure him as I send the hospital a text message asking for a sexual assault team to be on standby.

DeAndre starts to gag a little. "I don't know if I'll ever be able to be with a girl. The whole idea of someone touching me makes me sick to my stomach."

"All of this is brand-new right now. You haven't even had a chance to process it. It all takes time. There are counselors who specialize in helping people recover from traumas like the one you experienced. I have a good friend who was kidnapped for five years and experienced many of the same things you did. If you don't mind, I can put you in touch with him and he can help you find some resources."

"Do you think your friend can help make my nightmares go away? Every time I close my eyes for even just a second, I smell that guy's breath on my neck. I can't eat, I can't sleep… I can't even think right anymore. How can I go back to school? I miss my friends but I'm not the person I was a month and a half ago." DeAndre angrily wipes tears out of his eyes. "I don't even remember who I was back then." He struggles to draw a breath as he lets out a sob. His eyes dart around the room. "You're not recording this, are you?"

"No, you're not a suspect. You're a crime victim. We're going to get some help. But your brother is right — the sooner we can get you tested at the hospital, the better. The team who is meeting us at the hospital is extremely professional. They know what they're doing and they'll make this as painless as they possibly can."

"They won't think I'm a wimp because I didn't fight back and stop him?"

"No, no one will judge you for that. Many of the nurses have been through similar experiences. I'm not sure who the SANE nurse is today, but I wouldn't be surprised if it's Ryan Griffith. He is a great nurse. He understands what it's like to go through trauma because he was captured and held briefly as a prisoner of war."

"Guess I'm not the only person with crappy luck. What's a SANE nurse? I don't think I'm crazy yet, even though some days I feel like it."

We walk out to my car and get in before I finish my answer. I elect to take my personal car instead of the squad car since DeAndre has an aversion to law enforcement. "Ryan definitely had more than his share of bad luck, but he was able to bounce back. SANE is just a fancy acronym for a Sexual Assault Nurse Examiner. Ryan is a forensic nurse and he's received special training to conduct sexual assault evidentiary exams for rape victims."

"Can you say that in English for me?"

"When you get to the hospital, you'll be assigned a nurse — maybe it'll be Ryan, maybe not — who is specially trained to handle sexual assault cases. They will ask you questions in a way that will collect as much information as possible so prosecutors will have a chance to bring your assaulter to justice. They'll also collect as much physical evidence as they can."

DeAndre grimaces. "So, my brother was right — they're going to poke and prod me and take all sorts of pictures of me? Do I have to be naked in front of all those people? Can they knock me unconscious with some medicine or something — you know like they do at the dentist? I don't want another horrible memory. The ones I have are bad enough —"

"I'm sorry, I wish they could do it that way, it would be much easier for victims. Unfortunately, they can't because they need your input. They have to know what you went through. We have to document everything that happened to you for the case against the sexual offender. That's how we're going to catch this creep. They have to take pictures. But what I can tell you is they won't ask you to parade around naked in front of the whole hospital. It's done in a very respectful way. The SANE nurse will collect as much DNA as possible. Hopefully there'll be some."

For the first time tonight, DeAndre smiles. "Actually, I think there will be. That's how I got away."

I look at him with a puzzled expression and DeAndre explains. "You remember a while back when I was attacked with a knife when I tried to leave the gang life?"

I nod. "I remember. They glued your skin together, right?"

"Yeah, it left a gnarly scar on my chest. Anyway, when I told the investor guy I was a virgin, he was like totally stoked. He stopped using condoms. Then he noticed the scar on my chest. I told him it was because I had a blood transfusion and I showed him the scars on my legs from the time I was shot. I told him I had AIDS. He beat the crap out of me but he threw me out of the hotel and onto the street. I walked to the Greyhound station. I was totally stupefied when I learned I was in Sarasota and not Jacksonville. I took the bus back home. My mom wasn't home, but Dashonte was and he brought me right to you guys."

"That was a genius strategy to get away. I'm impressed you thought of it."

"Yeah, I don't know why I didn't think of it like the first week I was kidnapped."

"Sometimes, you have to wait for the opportunity to present itself, but you did great. You should be proud of yourself," I insist.

"I bet you say that to everyone you help," DeAndre says.

"Actually, I don't. What you did was pretty extraordinary. You need to own this one."

DeAndre shoots me a shy grin. "You know, you're an okay guy for a cop. Do you think you could stay with me while they do whatever they're going to do? I mean, I've already told you my whole story. So, it's not like you don't already know. I'd kinda like to have a friend there."

"I'll see what I can do to make it happen."

After I dropped DeAndre off and he ran into the very

grateful arms of his mother, I was finally able to check my messages. I smiled when I saw one from Tori. She sent me a selfie with flour on her face. It was captioned, "There'll be a surprise for you at my house whenever you're ready. Come see me."

I try to slink into the house without waking up Calico Jack because it's late. On Tori's kitchen table, I see a big bowl of peach cobbler next to a big thermos of what I presume to be coffee. It didn't take Tori long to learn exactly how I like my cuppa joe. Unlike Dylan, I like my coffee with a bucket load of cream and sugar. Tori fixes it just right. After I told her about my childhood memories of my grandmother living in a peach orchard in Georgia, Tori took it upon herself to learn how to make peach pie and peach cobbler just like my MawMaw used to make.

When I open the refrigerator to grab a glass of milk, I notice Tori has whipped some fresh cream to go with the peach cobbler. I take it out of the refrigerator and set it down on the table as I go in search of my beautiful chef.

I find her in the bathroom wearing her pajamas and fuzzy slippers, tying a bandanna over her hair. I stand behind her and kiss her on the back of her neck. "The peach cobbler looks delicious, thank you. But I don't want to eat it alone. Come eat with me please."

She giggles. "That tickles." She rubs her stomach. "I really shouldn't. I've been snacking along the way."

"Oh come on. I don't want to eat all that by myself! You're perfect the way you are. You know cobbler is irresistible."

She chews on her bottom lip indecisively. "Okay, I'll

have a little," she capitulates easily. "It smells too good to resist."

"It does smell great. It's exactly what I needed," I comment as I walk hand-in-hand with her to the kitchen.

"How are you? Your call took a while. I wanted to stay up, but I finally gave up and decided to go to bed."

I hug her close to my side and admit, "Today is one of those days where I both love and hate my job."

"Yeah? Did it turn out to be DeAndre?"

"It did. The poor kid has been through hell. It has him questioning who he is and whether he'll ever be the same. I don't have answers to those questions. Like in the case of Isadora, the experience has fundamentally changed who DeAndre will be going forward. He asked me several times how he goes back to being the person he used to be — I didn't know how to find the words to tell him he probably won't ever make it back to being the kid he once was."

"I'm sorry you had to be put on the spot. You don't really have the training and expertise to share that news with him. It's life altering. It should have been a psychologist or something."

"He'll have those people involved too. He's got a great SART team involved at the hospital. I'm grateful Ryan is part of his team because he's been through some trauma himself. The reality of the situation is that for some reason DeAndre trusts me. We've built some sort of rapport and I don't want to break that trust by being less than honest with him. So, I had to tell him the truth — as hard as it was."

Tori wraps her arms around my neck and pulls my face closer to hers. She brushes a kiss across my lips. "I'm sorry. But as hard as it is on you, it's a great sign that he asked you to tell him the truth. It means he trusts you. If he didn't, he would ask you to tell him what made him feel good. We've all dealt with clients who want us to tell them a fairytale so they can continue to stay in their little bubble. As painful as it is, at least he's making progress toward healing."

"Tori, I have to tell you, the truth is awful. DeAndre has years of counseling in front of him, and he was just beginning to get his life back on track. It seems so unfair. His grades were finally good enough where he might have actually gotten some scholarships and now it's not even certain he'll be in good enough shape to go back to school." I scrub my hand down my face and wipe tears away. "Geez! Sometimes I hate my job!"

Tori steps out of my arms and grabs a paper towel from the counter. She comes over and gently wipes my face. She lingers to give me a slow, thorough kiss. Tori grabs my peach cobbler from the table along with my thermos. She walks over to the couch and sets it on the coffee table. "Be right back," she says. She opens the kitchen cupboard and gets another bowl down and dishes up some peach cobbler for herself. She pours some coffee from the coffee maker on the counter into a mug and dumps a little sugar into it. Tori motions for me to join her as she carries her peach cobbler and coffee over to the couch and sits down. She takes a sip of her coffee and then sets it on the coffee table beside my thermos.

"I didn't mean to keep you up. It's late." I protest as she takes a few bites of her cobbler.

She shrugs. "It's not as if I have places to go and people to see. I was planning to be up for you anyway."

"I could get used to coming home to you every day.

I could easily get addicted to this little habit." I confess.

"I think it's too late for me. I'm already addicted to you. I know why you hate your job right now. But I also understand why DeAndre trusts you with his deepest secrets. You're passionate about your job, it's obvious you care and you do your best to tell the truth. I think people can sense that. I know the current situation is tough, but remember it could be much worse. Think about what would've happened if you hadn't been there for DeAndre. He might not even have felt brave enough to come forward and be honest and forthright about what happened to him. You would've lost all the evidence against his perpetrator and that would have been disastrous. As painful and awkward as it is, count yourself lucky you can establish that kind of relationship with the people you serve."

"You're right. I've been trying to build up trust with DeAndre and his family for over five years. I guess my patience finally paid off. I'm mentally fried. Sadly, we're only halfway through this job — there are still two more missing kids."

"Did DeAndre have any information about them?"

I shake my head. "No, he was too fragile today. I didn't even broach the subject. I figured it was a topic better addressed another day. DeAndre's number one job today was to get through a forensic sexual assault exam."

Tori snuggles against my chest. "No one should ever have to endure one of those … or witness it. In my book, you guys are both my heroes."

"You won't get any argument from me. I just wish we lived in a world where exams like that were no longer necessary."

CHAPTER EIGHTEEN

TORI

"Mom, do you want more sugar in your tea?" I ask as the waitress brings a refill of my mom's drink.

"I didn't have tea. I was drinking strawberry soda," my mom insists.

Fortunately, this little mom-and-pop restaurant is close to the rehab facility and we are frequent visitors, so they are used to my mom's lapses in memory. The waitress squats down next to my mom's wheelchair. "Oh, I'm sorry Miss Velma, we're out of strawberry soda. Would you like to try orange?"

My mom wrinkles her nose. "I don't like orange soda. I think I'll just have iced tea. May I have a lemon slice?"

The waitress smiles and nods as she takes the lemon slice off the edge of the glass she just delivered to the table and puts it back on. "Is this all right Ms. Velma?"

"Oh, that's perfect dear. My daughter always forgets what I like to drink."

The waitress pats me on the shoulder as she walks around to my side of the table. "Can I get you ladies some pie?"

"You should get Valerie peanut butter pie. She's too skinny."

My heart breaks just a little. For a while, it seemed like the new medication was helping my mom, but she's forgotten my name again.

I smile up at the waitress with tears in my eyes. "My name is Victoria, but most folks call me Tori. I'd like a piece of peach pie please."

My mom looks at me with surprise. "Don't be silly. You never eat fruit pie. When you were a child, you always said it was too sour."

Her words are like a thousand paper cuts. In the weird way that memory works when someone has dementia, she can't remember my name or my phone number, but she remembers I didn't like fruit when I was a kid. It just doesn't seem fair.

"You're right, Mom. When I was in kindergarten, I didn't like peach pie, but I'm older now. I like it fine these days."

My mom's complexion turns a little gray. "I changed my mind. I'm not hungry anymore. I want to go lay down."

"What's wrong? Is it your hip? Are you in pain? Do you need some medication?" I rattle off questions as I try to figure out what's wrong.

"No, child, I'm just tired of you. I want you to leave me alone."

I sit back in my chair, stunned by her mercurial mood swing.

I struggle to hold myself together as I quietly pay our bill and escort my mom back to the rehabilitation center and tearfully tell her goodbye — although she seems to have disappeared to a place where she doesn't remember who I am again.

I can't even begin to drive home because my tears are nearly blinding me. I move my car to a secluded corner of the parking lot and sob. When I envisioned my later years with my mom, I thought about vacations at Disney, painting classes, and cruises. I never thought there would be times I would rejoice when my mother remembered my name, or weeping on days where she would beg me to leave her alone.

When I pick up my phone to text Cody, I jump a couple of inches in the air when it rings in my hand. The number says Identity Bank West, so I answer it immediately, despite my state of dishevelment. My heart is still racing when I answer, "Hello? This is Victoria."

"Umm, hi, this is Phoenix Wolf, Tristan Macklin wanted me to give you a call."

Immediately, I sit up straighter and turn the volume up on my phone. "Is there a problem? Is Cody okay?" I ask as a terrible thought crosses my mind.

"Oh, I'm sorry. I didn't mean to frighten you. As far as I know, there's nothing wrong with Detective Erickson. This is about the videotape Mr. Macklin asked me to evaluate for you."

"I apologize, I'm in a very strange mood today. Cody is in the middle of a difficult operation at work and I'm worried about him."

"I'm aware. That's why Tristan has been working on this project. I'm gifted at detail work. Mr. Macklin and Mr. Roguen have been helping local law enforcement with the kidnapping case, so they handed your case off to me — I hope you don't mind," he stammers awkwardly.

"Just a moment please," I reply as I take a napkin from my glove compartment and blow my nose. "Sorry, I've had a rough day. No, of course I don't mind. I wasn't expecting the head of the company to take on my case. I'm grateful for any help I can get."

"Okay. I'm happy to help. Do you mind if I give you a verbal report over the phone, or do you want me to come to the Florida office to report in person? I'll be issuing a written report you can take to law enforcement, if you'd like."

"Oh, wow! You found that much? Do you think we need to talk in person?"

"Not really, some of our clients just expect that kind of service," Phoenix explains.

"I see." My mind is going through a million different scenarios, each more dire than the last. "Okay, can you just give me the highlights now, so I don't cause myself to have an aneurysm when I think about all the things you could've found on the tape. I'm in my car right now but I would love to hear more later when I can take notes and maybe have my boyfriend with me. He can be more objective about it all."

Phoenix chuckles softly. "I've met Cody. I don't know if he can be more objective when it comes to you, but it wouldn't hurt to have another opinion about all this."

Something about his dry tone makes me laugh too. "Okay, you have a good point — but, I'd still like Cody to hear what you have to say. So, what did you find?"

"Well, there are a couple of things. First, the raw

video Kat Burns provided to Tristan is not the same as the video which was provided to the news outlets."

"You're kidding! I was totally bluffing when I told Derek Zane the same thing. He got under my skin that day because he was being a patronizing jerk. I was trying to call his bluff and see if he would tell me why in the heck he fired me. I had nothing on him, but I decided to go all in because I didn't have anything to lose. He'd already fired me from my job — I figured he couldn't do much more." I laugh bitterly. "I guess I was wrong. The jerk filed a bar complaint against me. Can you believe that?"

"Well, he might not be the only jerk in your life —" Phoenix says mysteriously. "We were able to chase down the so-called anonymous tips to several media outlets. Tristan has worked with local news stations many times and helped solve several high-profile cases. One of the new stations gave him a copy of the tape where the person was bragging about having the tape of you in the elevator. Tristan figured if the person was bragging in one location, they probably bragged somewhere on social media. He has a computer program which analyzes voice messages. We use this program to catch people who catfish."

"Fascinating, but what does this have to do with my case?" I ask.

"You may be interested in hearing who the computer program matched the voice file with — Or would you rather wait until I give the full report?"

"I think you know the answer," I practically growl with impatience.

"Well, this result surprised me so much, I ran the

program three more times with different samples to confirm the finding."

"Please don't tell me it's somebody I know —" I plead with the sense of foreboding.

"I suppose it's possible you know him. I don't know how connected you are to local politics. The computer did a voice analysis and matched with an eighty-seven percent degree of accuracy to a gentleman named Shaddick Warren."

"Shut the front door!" I exclaim.

"I've never really understood that expression," Phoenix says.

"Me neither, but it saves me from saying vastly inappropriate stuff. You're pretty sure it's him?"

"Like I said, I ran multiple samples. They averaged out to eighty-seven point four percent. Is this consistent with what you know of the councilman?"

"Considering his girlfriend was promoted into my position, I'd say so," I retort, not hiding my disgust.

Phoenix is silent for a couple of moments and I wonder if I went too far. Through my phone, I hear him shuffling papers. "That's interesting," he finally says. "Our records show the councilman's been married for twelve years and has two daughters aged ten and seven."

"Somehow that doesn't even shock me. It makes me profoundly sad for his family, but it doesn't surprise me."

"You're sure they're not simply colleagues?"

"I have no first-hand knowledge, but my good friend still works there. The other day she went to deliver a fax to the new prosecutor who is allegedly the Councilman's girlfriend. She didn't even realize they were in the office so she entered Stacy's office without an invitation and caught them in a compromising position right in the middle of the day. They didn't even bother to lock the office door."

"Huh, do you think your friend would be interested in talking to Isaac Roguen? Just so our file is complete as to motive?"

"In a heartbeat. Crystal has been waiting for someone to listen to her side of the story."

"Awesome! What's Crystal's last name? I'll text Isaac right now."

"It's Crystal Downing. She'll be happy to hear she has something to contribute. She was angry when she thought I had been unfairly discriminated against, but who knows how big this is?"

"That's what we aim to figure out Ms. Clarkson."

"I can't wait for Cody to hear what you found out. I'll call you when he's available to talk, okay?"

"Works for me. I'll text you my direct line. I'm sorry you're having a tough day. I hope what I told you makes it a little better."

"You have no idea how much better this makes me feel. Sure, it's a little disconcerting to know someone with the power of Councilman Warren is after me. On the other hand it makes me feel less crazy. I knew I did nothing wrong, but there was this tape out there which made it seem like I did. But, thanks to you, I can now refute his so-called evidence. Now I have a name and a face to put behind the effort to push me out of my job. It makes it a little more manageable."

"I know what you mean. When Zoe's brother was on the loose, we didn't know where he would strike next. We knew he was dangerous, but we didn't know how dangerous he was or if he would actually hurt Zoe. It was a horribly scary time. We felt stuck until we knew he was behind bars."

"You took the words right out of my mouth. I'm going to go home now and talk to Cody. I'll send you a text later and set up a time for us to have a video call so you can fill Cody in on all the details. I can't wait to nail this guy. Hey, do me a favor? My gut tells me he's not working alone. I still think my former supervisor Derek Zane is somehow tied in with Shad Warren. Those two guys are like two peas in a pod. They both give me the creeps and they are far too cozy for my comfort. I bet you they are working together. Derek Zane doesn't like me because I wouldn't feed his ego and go out with him. I can't imagine he would destroy my career for that, but stranger things have happened."

"Okay, I'll add the possibility to my notes and get back to you later."

"Phoenix, can I ask you a question?"

"Sure, I don't know if I'll be able to answer it — but I'll try."

"Do you think you'll be able to collect enough scientific evidence that he won't be able to buy his way out of this no matter how much money he has?"

"I don't know for certain, ma'am. But, we're certainly gonna give it a shot."

"I guess that's all I can reasonably ask for."

"Sometimes, a fair shot is all we really need."

I have my iPad set up on the coffee table between us. There is a large chicken pesto pizza there too, but I am too nervous to eat. I gave Cody a bit of the news, but he stopped me and told me that it would be better if he heard it directly from Phoenix.

He's so funny. He brought a whiteboard from his place to take notes on. It looks like the kind we had in school. It's so big that he had to borrow Dylan's pickup to bring it over to my house. He even bought a brand-new package of dry erase markers. When I asked him why he needed such an elaborate set up, he told me he wanted to be prepared for any breakthroughs in my case. His head will spin when he hears what Phoenix has to say.

I cringe when Cody pops another piece of pizza in his mouth. "Aren't you nervous? How can you eat at a time like this?"

"I have to eat. If I stopped eating every time a case made me anxious, I'd be a skeleton. Besides, this pizza is awesome. You should try some."

My stomach lurches at the suggestion. "No thanks. Maybe after all this is over."

Cody aims the iPad camera and glances over at me. "You ready? Let's see what Phoenix has to say. I've worked with him before. His girlfriend's brother is Katie's crazy ex. He did a good job of keeping Zoe safe. He's a little different, but his attention to detail is phenomenal. If anyone can put the puzzle pieces together, I think it's probably him."

"What he's found so far has been impressive, that's

for sure."

Cody links to Phoenix and I'm surprised to see a shaggy haired blonde guy wearing a plaid shirt. He has a pencil stuck behind his ear, and he's consulting a different monitor.

"Hey, Phoenix, how are you? Did we call it a bad time?"

Phoenix looks into the camera blankly. "Oh, no, this is fine. I was just chasing down some last-minute leads. Tori, you were right on about Zane and Warren. They are thick as thieves. My preliminary search of ties between them shows they go way back. They were fraternity brothers. It seems they have a penchant for dog racing and underground dogfights."

I sit up straight and stare intently into the camera. "You're kidding! No wonder Derek fought so hard when I tried to go after the puppy mill. He put up roadblocks every step of the way. At first, I thought he was simply acting as a good devil's advocate to make sure my case was strong but, in retrospect, I wonder if he was just trying to undermine my confidence and make me drop the case. He certainly wasn't happy when I won."

"I imagine not. It probably impacted his bottom line. I only have minimal information right now, but it looks like Warren and Zane were pretty active in online gambling pools in both dog racing and underground dogfighting."

"That's just sick," Cody mutters. "It doesn't matter how closely we monitor that stuff, it still happens right under our noses. I don't even want to tell you about the last rescue operation I went on with the Humane Society. I had nightmares for weeks."

"Well, that explains why my supervisor didn't view my big victory as something to congratulate me over. It may also provide his motivation to fire me. It might even explain why he manufactured evidence to get me fired and filed a bar complaint against me. What I don't get is what in the heck Shaddick Warren has against me? I barely know the man."

"Shaddick Warren is one messed up dude. I don't think it boils down to one thing. Like we discussed earlier, by all appearances, he's not only cheating on his wife, he orchestrated an unlawful firing to get his mistress a job. We weren't able to tell exactly how long this relationship has been going on, but we were able to uncover evidence that they've known each other at least three years," Phoenix answers.

"Oh great! I wonder if they've been plotting that long to push me out of my job?" I ask, feeling defeated. "It must've killed them when I was promoted into Mr. Fleming's position as assistant district attorney."

"I don't know. If we speculate on that, we're getting ahead of the evidence. We know Shaddick Warren is heavily in debt between his gambling debts and his campaign debts. We also know he's leading a double life. He presents himself as a wholesome family man, while he's privately carrying on a long-term affair."

"It's really not so private," I mumble under my breath. "Apparently, everyone in my former office knows about it."

"That may very well be true. At this point, we haven't investigated further to see who else is aware of their relationship."

"I'd be willing to bet if a few people know, several

other people are aware," Cody comments.

"I think so too. I haven't had a chance to deep-dive into Shaddick Warren's background but a preliminary search uncovered something disturbing which might also play into what's happening to you."

"What do you mean?" I ask with trepidation.

"I found several old social media posts from Shaddick Warren that he tried to bury when he ran for public office. Unfortunately, what you post on social media stays there forever. At the very least, Shaddick Warren sympathizes with white supremacist values. I have a hunch when I dig a little deeper, it might be more. Usually, when someone goes to the lengths Shaddick Warren did to hide their digital past, there is more to the story. It'll just take me a little time to find out the whole story."

"So, I just want to make sure I understand this correctly," Cody says as he stands up to write on the whiteboard. "From what Tori has told me, you discovered concrete evidence that the tape was tampered with and you now have evidence that two people conspired to wrongfully terminate her and smear her reputation in order to advance another person? Does Stacy have an active role in this scheme?"

"I'm not sure if Ms. Hildebrand helped commit any crimes or if she is just a lucky recipient of the windfall."

"I hate to be a wet blanket. I don't know if any of this will make any difference. The people who matter might decide it's just a nasty employment dispute and avoid it like the plague. If they do that, all this evidence means nothing."

Cody squeezes my arm. "You're not looking at the

picture through a wide enough lens. If everything Phoenix is saying is true, one of our newest politicians is involved in an elaborate scheme to perpetrate what amounts to a hate crime."

"Even if all that's true, it may not matter if I lose my battle to save my legal career. We're in a race against time. The State Bar is investigating as we speak."

"Don't worry. I'm on it. The report on the videotape is ready to go. The supplemental report on the relationship between Warren and Zane should be wrapped up in a couple of days. I venture to guess based on what we found, your license to practice law is safe."

I sag against Cody in relief. "You know, there were days in the middle of really tough trials I used to say that I hated my job and I wondered why I ever became an attorney. I take it all back. I'm sorry I ever said that. I'm proud of the work I do and I don't want anyone to take away my right to do it."

"I understand," Phoenix responds. "We're working as quickly as we can to rectify the situation."

"We really appreciate all that you're doing. Thank you for stepping up. Let us know if you need anything else from us," Cody says.

Phoenix smiles at Cody. "Will do. It will be a pleasure to help bring these guys to justice. I hate people who act like jerks just because they think they can get away with it."

"Me too, Phoenix. Me too." I respond, feeling hopeful for the first time in several weeks

CHAPTER NINETEEN

CODY

As Toby Payne sets up his presentation in the conference room, Dylan glances over at me with a skeptical look as he grabs a donut from the box. I just shrug. Toby may look young, but his skills are impressive. It's one of those things you need to see to believe, so I'll wait and let Toby dazzle Dylan on his own. Darya is watching the interplay between the two of us in silence waiting to see if she has to intercede. She's been on enough task force assignments with the two of us to know sometimes she needs to play referee.

Toby turns back to us and clears his throat. "I wanted you all here today because I think I made a breakthrough. Each of you has a missing persons case you are working, correct?"

"Well, Isadora isn't technically missing anymore but her perpetrator hasn't been caught yet," Darya clarifies.

"DeAndre isn't missing either, but he was. I have another potential missing teen. I'm still trying to rule out whether he left voluntarily."

Toby scowls at me. "Make that determination

carefully.”

“I will. After meeting you, I’ll never look at a missing child case quite the same ever again. In this case, the parents are insistent he’s simply rebelling against the rules but his grandmother isn’t so sure, so I’m looking a little closer before I decide.”

Dylan’s voice snaps with pent-up anger as he demands. “Do you have news on Tallulah Johnson? Her parents may have given up, but I haven’t.”

“That’s what I was getting to. I believe I found the connection between cases. With their permission, I examined the text messages both DeAndre and Isadora received from the YouTube promoter. I found they were both going to a site called The Ignis Fatuus Hex.”

Dylan shakes his head and chuckles wryly. Darya and I look at each other blankly trying to figure out what’s so funny. Toby grins at our confusion. “Did I mention both my parents are teachers? When I ran across this odd name for a YouTube channel, it sent chills up my spine. It’s almost as if this dude wanted to be caught. He gave clues about the nature of his website right in the name.”

“Sorry, you’ll need to be a little more explicit. I guess I wasn’t paying close enough attention in English class that day,” Darya admits.

Dylan sticks up his hand. “I’ve got this one. The words in the website name mean a delusion or a false hope combined with a curse.”

Darya’s eyes widen. “Wow! That’s putting it right out there if you know where to look. I take it no one looked?”

“Isadora and DeAndre thought his name was Ig. DeAndre figured it was some Hollywood name,” I add.

“How does the disappearance of Tallulah Johnson

fit into this?" Dylan asks as he takes notes on a legal pad.

"I'm not exactly sure, although my hunch is that she was probably snared by the same trap. DeAndre told us this Ignis person, who I believe to be Bex Michaels, specifically targeted kids who were shy, artistic types. If I remember correctly, Tallulah Johnson was involved in theater and choir, so the pattern would fit. However, I can't confirm my hunch until I have access to her computer records."

Dylan shoots out of his chair. "I can do better than get you records. I'll be right back." Dylan rushes out of the conference room.

"I'll check with Joey Ward's parents to see if I can get access to his phone or computer. Maybe we can see if he's tied in to the rest of the missing teens. It might help to determine whether he left voluntarily."

"That would be helpful. The more victims we can tie to one perpetrator, the stronger the case becomes."

"Speaking of the perpetrator, have we gotten any closer to finding him?"

"Not so far. I hope each new clue I uncover will bring me a little closer to something which will break the case wide open."

Dylan comes back into the conference room carrying a large evidence box. He pulls out a computer case with an evidence tag on it. "This is Tallulah Johnson's laptop. She took it everywhere with her. She wanted to major in journalism in college. She was on the school paper and she was always writing stories everywhere she went. After her parents had a funeral for her, they turned it over to us — in part to see if we could find any clues on it, but also because they couldn't bear to see it."

Toby's eyes light up. He digs around in his large presentation case and pulls out a pair of purple neoprene gloves and a new external hard drive. He opens Tallulah's laptop and plugs in the external hard drive. "I'm going to mirror her computer on this drive. You'll need her computer as pristine as possible for evidence in the trial. I can duplicate it on one of my machines."

"You're telling me you brought an extra computer just in case something like this happened?" Dylan asks skeptically.

"You've met my boss, Tristan Macklin, right?"

I smirk at Dylan. "He's right. He does work for Identity Bank. If Tristan thought we needed extra planes to search for these kids, they'd be parked out front with pilots on standby."

"Point taken," Dylan responds with a laugh. "So you can evaluate her laptop right here — you don't even have to take it?"

"I don't have to take her original computer, but it will take me a bit to download the data and upload it to my computer. Then I'll need to go through it."

"I hope this doesn't take months. Tallulah is running out of time if it's not already too late," Dylan remarks as he takes a bottle of antacids out of his pocket and downs a handful.

"With all due respect, Detective Palmer, I know that better than anyone in this room. I can't promise any miracles, but I will work on this as quickly as I can."

"Toby, we all know you're trying your best. Tempers are a little short around here," I comment as I level a steely glare at my former partner, "but we're all trying our best. Sometimes, we are so stressed out, it's hard to remember we're all playing on the same team."

"It's okay, I understand."

"Let us know when you know something. I'll try to get you the information from Joey Ward's computer too."

Dylan walks over and shakes Toby's hand. "Hey man, I'm sorry. My remarks were thoughtless. For a moment, I forgot who I was talking to."

Toby smiles shyly. "You know, that might be the nicest thing anyone's ever said to me. There was a time in my life I thought no one would ever forget the nightmare I've been through. I figured I would forever be known as the kid who went to the library and never came home. I never thought I'd be able to outgrow the stigma and move on with my life. The fact that you completely forgot that about me totally makes my day. Thanks Dylan. Means a lot."

"Let's go find some other kids before they've been missing for half a decade," Dylan says as tears threaten.

"That's the plan. I work on it every moment I'm awake. As you can tell, I don't sleep much these days either."

I clear my throat before I say, "I don't know about you guys, but I'm looking forward to solving this case so I can finally get a good nights' rest for a while."

Darya says, "From your lips to God's ears."

Tori clutches my hand and sticks it in the pocket of my pea coat as we stroll past the storefronts with their festive displays. "Thank you for dinner. It was lovely. I appreciate what you were trying to do. This waiting is driving me crazy. I still can't believe they deposed me. Usually I'm the one who gives the depositions."

"I'm sure you did fine. It was probably just a formality. They have to do the same process with everyone, otherwise they would be accused of bias."

"I know." Tori lays her head on my shoulder. "As far as deposition goes, it was pretty standard, but it was just weird being on the other end of things. I was trying to read the tea leaves to see if I could figure out where the investigation stood — but they weren't giving anything away. That was probably the most frustrating part of it all."

"So now you just have to wait for them to conclude their investigation? Did they give a timeframe?"

She shakes her head. "They said each investigation varies."

"Sounds like what's going on in my cases. I swear if I didn't have you around to keep me sane, I don't know what I would do."

Tori looks up at me in surprise. "Really? I don't know that I do all that much except add more chaos to your life."

"That's not true," I insist. "You add balance to my life. Not only have you pitched in and helped with this case when I need you, you're a great sounding board when I needed to vent, and a cheerleader when I'm down. You've kept me from living and breathing this case twenty-four seven and giving myself an ulcer because I drink nothing but coffee for months on end."

"That sounds like a lot. I thought you were the one rescuing me from my crazy life which was spiraling out of control."

"Maybe we just got our timing right this time." I place my arm around her waist and pull her closer. Tori stops in front of an elaborately decorated store window with vintage teddy bears and trains. "Oh my gosh! How adorable is this?" Then she looks up at me with tears in her eyes as she voices the thought rattling around in my brain. "Oh, those poor parents! It must be so hard for them to see all this Christmas stuff and not know where their kids are."

"I think about that every single day. I know Isadora does too. She calls me once or twice a week to see if there have been any new developments. It's been a hurry up and wait game for a while. It seems like we get a promising lead and chase it down, only to find out it wasn't so promising."

"I'm sorry. Is there anything I can do to help?" Tori asks.

I lean down and brush a kiss across her lips. "I guess the best strategy right now is for us to distract each other until we have news we can work with."

She stands on her tiptoes and threads her arms around my neck, pulling my face closer to hers as she kisses me deeply. "I can get on board with that strategy."

Chapter Twenty

Tori

As I sort through new leads in the missing teens case, my phone rings. I reflexively answer it without even looking. I catch my breath when an older gentleman greets me. "Hello, is this Victoria Clarkson?"

"This is." I respond with trepidation.

"Hello, my name is Humphrey Coche, I'm calling on behalf of the State Bar. I apologize it's taken us so long to get back to you. Normally, I would simply issue you a formal letter informing you of our findings. However, this case is so extraordinary, I feel a personal call is warranted."

My head spins and I feel faint. "Oh my, that does not bode well for me."

"Oh no, ma'am, I didn't mean to insinuate anything of the sort. Let me get that out of the way right up front. Our investigation found the allegations against you to be unfounded and meritless. As far as we are concerned, you remain a member of the Florida State bar in good standing."

I slump down in my chair as a wave of relief

overtakes me and twin feelings of relief and rage course through me. "I appreciate your thoughtful consideration of this matter," I reply as soon as I can calm my racing heartbeat enough to speak.

"But?" he prompts.

"It doesn't seem fair that I didn't do a single thing wrong, but whenever someone looks up my record, the blemish will always be there — even though it's been established that I was wrongly accused."

"You make a fair point, Ms. Clarkson. Given the unusual circumstances of this case, we are looking at ways to ameliorate the damage done."

"What does that even mean?"

"Well, ameliorate means to improve something perceived to be in a negative condition."

"While I appreciate the English lesson Mr. Coche, I wasn't asking for the definition of the word. I understand the meaning quite well. I am asking what will happen to my formerly spotless record."

"We're still working on what exactly will take place. Of course, our decision will be announced publicly. The question is how publicly. Typically, complaints are a relatively straightforward process and are used to protect the public from the unethical practice of law. However, in this case, it appears the complaint process was used as a means of sabotage and the executive board feels this is an egregious misuse of our process."

"Not surprisingly, I agree with your assessment. This experience has been very traumatic for me. If Mr. Zane filed a complaint simply to further destroy my career, he should have to face sanctions. That's not what you guys are here for. Whatever his issues are with me, he shouldn't have brought the Bar Association into it."

"Yes, that was our thought as well."

"So, what happens now?"

"We will release a formal statement exonerating you. Once we meet with our counsel to determine the proper way to deal with the unusual circumstances in this case. Of course, we are at liberty to release the name of the person who instigated the investigation — the question is how much we disclose of the surrounding circumstances. Mr. Zane's behavior has triggered an investigation into his fitness to serve as an attorney in the state of Florida."

I can't hold back my involuntary gasp. I always knew what Derek Zane did was underhanded and unethical, I just didn't expect anyone to ever hold him accountable.

My heartbeat sounds thunderously loud in my ears and I struggle to hear Mr. Coche as he continues, "However, until such time we decide how to handle this unusual case, I wanted to let you know the Disciplinary Committee takes this incident very seriously. We also view you as an innocent victim. We took a look at your admirable service to the state of Florida and we consider you an asset to the bar and hope you continue practicing in our state."

"Um, thank you, sir," I stammer. "I hope I get the opportunity to continue to practice law. My reputation has been shredded in the legal community and elsewhere. Starting over in Florida may not be possible."

"That's just a shame. Your record is stellar and should be celebrated."

"I appreciate your sentiment, I really do. Unfortunately, it will take a little more than a few pats on the back for people to forget what they've seen on the news day in and day out for months on end."

"It's a terrible thing. I'm sorry I can't right all the wrongs done to you. We will be looking into Mr. Zane to make sure he represents the kind of professionalism we want in our state."

"I know I wasn't a big fan of giving you a deposition before, but in this case, I would be more than happy to give the disciplinary committee whatever information you need," I offer. After a moment, I add, "Although if I file a complaint against Mr. Zane, it will look retaliatory."

"Oh, no worries, Ms. Clarkson. You don't have to initiate a complaint. There were enough concerns arising from our investigation, we have initiated the investigation ourselves," Humphrey Coche assures me.

"Oh," I blurt, unable to think of anything more sophisticated to say.

"Oh is right. Mr. Zane appears to have cooked his own goose. Were it not for his frivolous complaint against you, we would not have been aware of his allegedly unethical behavior."

"Huh, maybe that's why my mama always taught me to tell the truth and to keep my mouth shut if I couldn't say something nice about somebody."

Mr. Coche chuckles. "Obviously, your mother is a good woman. We deal with people every day who never got those lessons. I'm glad you're one of the people who obviously took those lessons to heart. I'll let you know if I need anything further from you Ms. Clarkson. I hope you find a way to repair your reputation and stay in Florida. It's been a delight to get to know you."

"Thank you for calling, Mr. Coche. It would not be

an overstatement to say you made my day."

"That's not something people usually say to me. I appreciate it. You have a good day now, Ms. Clarkson."

"Don't you worry, I plan to. Bye now."

As I stand silently in the doorway of the gym, I marvel at the strength and symmetry of Cody's muscles as he lifts free weights with Dylan. He's oblivious to my presence, so I take a few moments to watch the casual banter between two old friends. Cody laughs at a joke about last night's game and I have to catch my breath. The man is gorgeous. I can't believe we're finally making a go of it after all these years.

Dylan looks up and sees me in the doorway. He sets his barbells down and pokes Cody in the side. "Dude! You must be asleep or something. If I had a woman like that waiting for me, I wouldn't be sitting there jacking my jaw."

Cody whirls around with a shocked look on his face. "What are you doing here? Is everything okay with your mom?"

"Everything's fine. Actually, this time I tracked you down to share good news."

Cody wipes himself down with a towel from the weight bench. He stretches out his sore shoulder. "After the week we've been having, good news would be a welcome change. Hit me with it."

I can't contain my excitement anymore. I grin widely as I announce, "Well, you know what they say about karma —"

Cody jumps up from the weight bench and sprints toward me. "Hot dog! You heard from the bar —"

I nod. "Completely exonerated."

Cody stops a few feet from me. "I would give you a hug but I'm sweaty and I smell ripe."

"He's not kidding. I've been sitting a few feet from him and I can confirm his alibi. The man needs a couple of showers before he touches you," Dylan teases.

"Are you guys done? You're ruining my announcement. I didn't even get to tell you the best part," I pout.

"You mean there's more than being completely exonerated?" Cody asks.

"Oh, so much more. Derek Zane worked extremely hard to get me into trouble for something I didn't do — but he ended up getting himself into a world of hurt. The bar is launching its own investigation against him."

Dylan gives Cody a high five. "You didn't have to initiate it?"

I shake my head. "Nope. That's the beautiful thing. His behavior was so far out of bounds, the disciplinary committee found cause to look into his conduct as an attorney."

Cody leans down and carefully kisses me. "Wow, that is cause for celebration! Let me grab a quick shower and we can get out of here."

I stop grinning long enough to return the kiss. "Do you have to go back to work?"

Cody glances over at Dylan. "We good?"

"Yeah, Man. Go take your girl out and celebrate. Anything I come up with can wait until tomorrow. Get your stinky self in the shower before Tori changes her mind."

Cory throws his towel at Dylan. "Okay… I'm going … no need to be rude." He turns back toward me and winks. "Try to keep him out of trouble."

Dylan throws his head back and laughs. "Get real. She's been dating you long enough to know that's not even possible."

"Good point. Maybe I should've told you not to chase her away."

"Why would I do that? You eat at her house now. I'm saving a bundle on my grocery bill. This is a win-win for me."

"Glad to see you're so supportive of us —" Cody replies with an eye roll.

"If you don't go take your shower, I'll go on a date with your girlfriend. I've been hitting a dry spell lately. I could use a little fun in my life."

"I'm confident my girlfriend is too smart to fall for that line."

"You can stand around and joke all day, but I've got two words for you to consider, Cody —"

"Yeah? Whatcha got?" he challenges with a smirk.

"Crab Shack," I retort as I dangle my car keys in front of my face.

Cody spins on his heel and runs toward the shower. "'Nuf said. I'll be out in a minute."

As soon as he leaves the room, Dylan looks at me with wide-eyed wonderment. "What's so magical about the Crab Shack?"

I sigh softly. "I guess you had to be there. Cody and I have some unfinished business. Our last date got interrupted when you found Isadora. Maybe lightning will strike twice."

"As much as I would hate to interrupt your celebration, worse things could happen."

"If we could find Joey and Tallulah, that would be the ultimate celebration. I wouldn't mind that outcome at all."

"Well, you seem to be on a first name basis with karma these days, maybe you could put in a good word."

Cody hugs me to his chest as we watch the bonfire burn. "You know I'm torn."

"Yeah? Why?"

"It's hard for me to quit my day job."

"Hmm … I see. Warm, beautiful, romantic, nostalgic … and illegal without a permit, right?"

I feel Cody nod against the top of my head.

"I know, but look at them. They're having such a good time. Playing music and dancing — they're not hurting anybody. Don't you remember what it was like to be young?"

Cody spins me around and kisses me deeply. "Yeah, I do. That's why I don't want them to get in trouble," he replies reluctantly after he pulls away. "Paying fines out of your allowance or gas money sucks."

I run my hand down his cheek. "Okay, I'll be the bad guy this time."

I jog across the sand to the group of kids who seem to be the leaders and introduce myself. "Hey, I know my boyfriend and I seem like old fuddy-duddies to you. But we're simply trying to save you from a world of hurt. I don't know if you know this or not, but bonfires here are illegal."

"Giovanni, you said you got a permit," a tall brunette says.

The kid shrugs. "I say a lot of things. If I told you the truth, we wouldn't be having this banging party."

I grimace. "As far as I know, they don't issue permits for this beach. You might want to put it out before you guys get caught."

Giovanni draws himself up to his full height and challenges me, "What are you? The fun police?"

I reach down and brush some sand off my calf. "Just trying to be nice. If we were the fun police, this would have been handled much differently. Have a nice night."

I jog back over to where Cody is standing. He puts his arm around me and whispers in my ear. "Smart and classy. Way to diffuse a tense situation, Counselor."

"I hope they take our advice, but it's not our fight. Besides, we're here to celebrate the fact that I actually get to stay in the legal profession. No need to put that in jeopardy."

We reach Cody's Mustang and he backs me up against it and puts his arms around me. "Well, we've eaten the best seafood on the coast, cuddled a little on the beach and been the grumpy grown-ups. So, what's next?"

I pull his face toward mine and place a line of kisses down his jaw. "I don't know exactly. I just know this is the part of the date where I spill my guts. I tell you all the things I've been afraid to say over the last few months."

Cody captures my lips and kisses me deeply. He pulls away and helps me into his car. "Sounds serious. Let's get some place a little more private." He pulls the car behind some utility buildings on the edge of the parking lot and puts up his sun visor. "That's better."

I swallow hard. "I was feeling braver a few minutes ago. For someone who makes a living persuading people about matters of life and death, I find conversations like this remarkably tough."

Cody grabs my hand and kisses the back of it. "Come on, it's only me. I'm not that scary."

"Actually, this whole thing is scary. Remember when I told you my dad passed away when I was in elementary school? I often wonder if that was the beginning of my mom's dementia. It's almost as if her mind couldn't cope with the loss. I was young, but I still remember my mom's world completely falling apart. It's as if she lost her whole identity. Everything my mom did before my dad died, they did as a couple. They took dancing lessons and were part of a couples bowling league in their church. With my dad gone, my mom didn't know who she was anymore — even so, she had to pull herself together for me. The lesson I learned from all of that is you can't trust someone to stay around in your life."

"That's a harsh lesson. Probably not what your mom intended you to draw from the situation."

"Oh, definitely not. My mom loved my dad with a fierce passion. Before she got sick, she always talked to me about finding somebody just like daddy. The sad thing is I found you and she'll never know. In all the craziness of my life where people were literally out to destroy me, you were there by my side like a knight in shining armor slaying all the nasty dragons in my life."

"Babe, first of all, you've slayed a few dragons for me too. It's not as if you're some helpless damsel in distress. You've been kickin' some serious butt and taking names — I've just been cheering you on from the sidelines. Secondly, I think Velma does know who I am to you. She might not know from week to week whether I'm your milkman or the night nurse, but she calls me your young man. I believe that among all the lost thoughts in her mind, she knows that I love you and will always protect you."

I look up at him with teary eyes. "You jumped the gun, Cody Erickson. That's what I was trying to tell you — despite all the insane stuff we've been through in the last few months, I've fallen in love with you. You're everything I always dreamed of but was always afraid to go after. You tipped the scales. Love finally wins over injustice."

Cody struggles to get close enough to pull me into an embrace. "Until this very moment, I loved this car. Now I wish I had Dylan's gas-guzzling pickup," he mutters under his breath.

I lean over and Cody rewards me with a long, lingering kiss. "What do you know? I think we finally nailed the timing."

The words no sooner leave Cody's lips than his cell phone chirps with a ring tone I recognize as the one assigned to Dylan.

"This better be important —" he grumbles. "His timing sucks."

"That's what you said last time … answer your phone," I urge.

Cody puts his phone to his ear and listens for a brief moment before he shouts, "Son of a —" He straightens up and puts his seatbelt on. Following suit, I quickly buckle mine. "We'll be there as quickly as we can. Make sure the captain doesn't blow a gasket. It's not good for his heart."

Cody starts the car and throws it into drive as he peels out of the parking lot. "What happened?" I ask, when I catch my breath.

Cody glances over at me with a grim expression. "I can't believe I have to cut another date short. I wanted to celebrate our love story with you, but our rookie cop just got arrested."

"You're kidding! Pauline? The one we took with us last month when we went out with Jade and Declan and Stuart and Darya to sing karaoke?"

"The very same," he confirms.

"I thought you told me Pauline is one of the best rookies you've ever worked with?"

"*She is!*" Cody insists. "That's why Dylan says the captain is about to implode. I don't understand what happened."

Chapter Twenty-One

Cody

By the time I finally drop Tori off and get back to the station, Pauline is sitting in the corner of the dressing room tying her sweats and putting on her tennis shoes. Her face is freshly scrubbed, and she looks about twelve years old. Usually when she sees me, she has some smart aleck remark about my gray hair but today all she does is stare at me with tear-filled eyes. "Want to talk about it?"

She shakes her head. "I can't. I have to give a statement in a minute to tell you why I did what I did. But I need the captain and who knows who else out there first."

"Oh, it's already that serious? You must've stepped in it bad."

"Well, until a few minutes ago, I was wearing prison orange, if that tells you anything," she answers in a trembling voice.

"Good point. You know me, I won't form an opinion until I've actually heard what happened. I know you're a solid cop with good instincts. I'm certain you haven't changed overnight."

She smiles weakly. "Thanks. That means a lot. See you in there."

As I grab my cup of coffee and a pastry and take a seat, my captain walks by me and mutters, "Can you believe this garbage? I'll be filling out paperwork until retirement."

He sits down two chairs away. "There has to be a logical explanation. Pauline is smart. She's not your typical rookie. Let's not jump to all the wrong conclusions."

The captain looks at me and raises an eyebrow. "You got a reason for sticking up for her? Maybe a personal one?"

"No! I just think she's a solid cop. We should give her the benefit of the doubt, that's all I'm saying."

The captain rolls his eyes. "Whatever. That still doesn't fix my paperwork problem."

Pauline comes in to the briefing room and sits down on the stool. All eyes are on her. "First, I want to apologize. I did this op totally backwards, and it cost our agency some credibility — but the opportunity came up and I had to take it."

"What op?" Dylan presses.

Pauline's jaw goes slack in amazement. "Are you freaking kidding me? Did the Feebees not even brief you guys?"

The captain leans forward in his chair. "Brief us about what? We were told you were caught up in some prostitution sting."

"No, that's not exactly right. It wasn't prostitution at all — or at least not in the traditional sense of the word. I was caught up in a human trafficking sting. I was there because I put myself there. And I have good news I —"

"You did what? Without backup?" I roar.

"Okay, in retrospect it wasn't the best plan. I found Bex Michaels … but he was about to get away. So I had to make myself bait."

"Are you crazy? You made yourself bait for a known pedophile without any radio communication or backup?" I clarify.

"It was a spur-of-the-moment decision. I figured he could lead me to the other hostages."

"I take that back. I'm going to die while I'm filling out paperwork," the captain says as he scrubs his hand down his face. "Were you aware of the feds operation, at least?"

Pauline looks down at her tennis shoes. "If I was a good liar, I would probably tell you I knew all about it and that I was merely helping them. Unfortunately, I didn't. I was just focused on trying to get the guy who took DeAndre and Isadora. I was hoping he could lead me to Tallulah and Joey. I could see him getting away before I had a chance to get a formal operation together. For better or for worse, I followed my gut. I pretended to be a teenager who knew all about his website. I played fan girl, and he bought my act. Fortunately, I wanted to be a country music star when I was a kid. I play the guitar reasonably well and can sing a few songs off the top of my head. So he bought my whole cover story that I wanted to go to Nashville to become a singer."

Something about Pauline's demeanor strikes me. "Guys, I think we're missing the big headline here. Officer Lawrence, where the Feds able to recover any of the missing teens?"

Pauline nods vigorously. "Yes, Two teens resembling Tallulah Johnson and Joey Ward were recovered safely and Bex Michaels was arrested in the process — along with a bunch of his cohorts."

The captain's bushy eyebrows climb his forehead. "Nobody bothered to tell me anything … and I have families calling me every few hours. It would've been nice to know. By the way, next time you give a report about a rogue operation, you might want to lead with the most positive headline."

"Yes, Sir! Does this mean I'm not fired?" Pauline asks as she pushes her dark hair out of her face.

"Not so fast!" the captain snaps. "You violated more policies and regulations than I care to count — but we have bigger issues to deal with right now. I would advise you to sit yourself behind a desk and make yourself as useful as humanly possible until we get this sorted."

"But —" Pauline interrupts.

"But what, Rookie?" The captain scowls at Pauline, making it clear he didn't expect her to have anything to say about the matter. Even I am shaking in my boots at his expression and I've worked for the man for more than a decade.

"Tallulah and Joey were not the only kids found. The agency located nine other teenagers."

"I want you to make it your business to figure out how to contact those kids' parents as quickly as you can. Who knows how long they've been waiting?"

"Yes, Sir."

The captain glances over at me. "Erickson, don't you know some sort of computer whiz who can help Lawrence find the parents?"

"I do. I suspect Toby could work rings around us. Since time is critical, it makes sense to bring him in."

"Bring in your clerical assistant too. I've never seen your reports so organized. We'll need her help to stay on top of this. In the meantime, I need to figure out why our agency was excluded from the loop."

Dylan stands up and levels an odd look at the captain. "All things considered, I think I'd rather trade jobs with you. I have to go tell a family who thought their child was dead and gone that she's alive, but I don't know how extensive the torture was because the feds are still debriefing her. I'm not looking forward to this conversation. Something tells me the parents would almost rather pretend their daughter was dead than acknowledge all the potential horrific things she's probably been through."

The captain swings his head around to acknowledge the rest of the room before he scowls at Dylan. "Palmer, with all due respect, I have been on the receiving end of one of those death notices. Whatever hell the Johnson family has gone through, it is nothing compared to actually receiving a death notice. As upset as they currently are, they will feel much better once they are able to see an all there, living, breathing young lady. Even with all the wires and machines she is likely to be hooked up to, her presence in the hospital bed is far better than visiting her at the cemetery as they bury her."

Dylan blanches as he stuffs his hands in his pockets

and looks down at the floor. "Sorry, my mistake. I know better than to make assumptions."

"It's okay." Captain Schumaker glances over at Pauline. "Palmer, Erickson and Nelson, I need you to stay behind with Officer Lawrence. Everyone else get back to work. Everything we've been doing just got kicked into high gear." Pauline, Dylan and I sit around the table shuffling papers and feeling anxious as everyone piles out the briefing area. After everyone has gone, the captain makes a huge show of closing the doors behind them. When he's finished, he turns around toward Pauline and says, "This is one hundred percent off the record and not to be repeated. Does everyone understand?" We all look at each other and nod.

The Captain lets out a deep breath as we watch the last of the group file out of earshot, he glances over at Pauline. "I'm sorry the rules are what they are — but I want to say something to you privately. Whatever comes of this publicly, I want to thank you. You displayed great instincts. We can argue all day about whether it was prudent, or within policies and regulations — but at the end of the day, you saved nearly a dozen children and teenagers. It's more than we at this office have been able to do in over a year. Good on ya. After this conversation today, I have to go back to doing my job and complying with rules and regulations to help keep you safe. But unofficially, I'm incredibly proud of the job you did for those kids in our department. Hopefully, when I have to act in my official capacity, I'll be able to come to the same conclusion."

Pauline swallows hard and dabs away tears. "Thank you sir, I appreciate your support."

"Now, for the rest of you, let's go do our jobs. We've

got families to unite, evidence to collect and witnesses to talk to. I don't want this perp to slip through our fingers again. Let's cross all our T's and dot all our I's."

"Consider it done," I pledge as I grab one of notebooks and start to make myself a list of things which need to be done.

Dylan is uncharacteristically quiet on the drive over to the Johnson's house. I've been on assignments often enough with him to know to simply leave him be when he's in this kind of mood. Finally, he blurts, "That was a gutsy move from Lawrence. Stupid as all get out — but gutsy."

"It sure was — but don't even pretend it's not something you or I would've done as rookies. We always tried to come up with ways to do things better than our training officers. This is exactly the kind of stunt we would've pulled back then. Heck, there's nothing to say we wouldn't do something like this now if we had the kind of break Pauline got. I can't say for certain if Bex Michaels was sitting right in front of me and I had the opportunity to dip undercover I wouldn't have taken it."

"I know. I guess that's part of the reason why it's so frustrating. I know she will get her butt handed to her for something any of the rest of us probably would've done. She probably should too, because it was a breach of protocol and she could've gotten killed — on the other hand, it was ingenious and solved the case," Dylan muses.

"I hope they take the ultimate outcome into account when they mete out her punishment, that's all I'm saying."

As we pull up in front of the Johnsons' home, Dylan

leans his head back against the headrest and presses his fingers into his eyeball sockets. "I have to tell you. I never, ever thought we would be having this conversation. Once the parents decided to have the funeral, I wondered if maybe the parents were right and I was just chasing pipe dreams. I've never been so glad to be wrong in my life."

Dylan and I walk up on the porch and awkwardly wait for someone to answer the door. I wonder how Dylan plans to approach this conversation. He has grown exceptionally close to this family and unlike many of the families we've been working with, this family was convinced their daughter had been the victim of foul play.

The door flies open. Mr. Johnson grabs Dylan by the waist and spins him around. "Detective Palmer, I should have listened to you. You said my Tallulie was alive, but I couldn't see it. I put my wife through the pain of burying an empty coffin. I'll never forgive myself."

After Mr. Johnson puts him back on the porch, Dylan takes a deep breath and tries not to favor his sore rib where a suspect landed a roundhouse kick a few weeks back. "It's been a hard time for everyone. It's hard to know how these cases will turn out. Tallulah was gone for a long time. I don't blame you for believing the worst had happened. Have you had a chance to talk to your daughter?"

Mrs. Johnson steps forward and hugs Dylan. "Yes, thank goodness! Tallulah is fine and she's on her way home." Mrs. Johnson steps back and invites us into her living room. Reluctantly, we sit on the pristine white couch in a room that looks like it was decorated for a fashion magazine. "She sounds so good. She says nothing bad happened to her. Can you believe an old man bought her to sing to his dying wife?”

I can't hide my surprise. "Really, that's it?"

"She says that's all that happened. She was terrified because the man's wife died and he was about to get rid of her when the FBI did the sting. She was rescued just in time," Mrs. Johnson explains as she wipes tears from her eyes. "Thank you for never giving up the search. You saved my daughter and so many others. There aren't enough words to express what it means."

"Thank you works for me," Dylan responds, his voice breaking with emotion. "I'm glad your daughter will be home safe. You have my number. Call me if you need anything."

Chapter Twenty-Two

Tori

Cody is still tying his tie when he comes out of my bathroom and sits down at the kitchen table. I don't know why he keeps his own place anymore. He practically lives here. I slide a couple of pieces of toast and a plate of scrambled eggs in front of him, along with some peach jam I made. I walk over and kiss him briefly before I ask, "How are things going with the investigation?"

"Toby is due back in Florida today to help Pauline match up families with the missing kids which were found. We tried to tell him we could do it remotely — but he wanted to be here."

"Any luck reaching Joey Ward's family?" I pour us some coffee and nibble on some toast.

Cody scrubs his hand down his face. "No, it's the strangest thing. No one can get a hold of them. It's like they disappeared off the planet. At first I thought we were just missing each other. I figured they were on their way to wherever Joey was being evaluated by the feds. Apparently, that's not the case. They've ghosted. This case has been weird from the beginning."

"I remember. It was the grandmother who was insistent he might be involved with your case, but the parents were reluctant to call you in, right?" I drink a few sips of my coffee. "What do you think that's about?"

"I don't know. Right now, I can't even get a hold of the grandmother. It's making the hair on the back of my neck stand up."

"This whole case has been a study in the bizarre. It seems like every kid who was taken was treated differently and abused differently —" I lose my train of thought as my phone rings. It's not the ring tone from the facility where my mom is staying. I breathe a small sigh of relief.

I glance down at the phone and notice it's Crystal. When I answer the phone, she screams loud enough Cody can hear it, "Turn the TV on!"

"What channel?" I ask.

"It doesn't matter. Any local news will do. Hang up and record it with your phone. Trust me you'll want to."

"This won't ruin my day will it?" I ask, concerned about the weird edge in her voice.

"No, I wouldn't do that to you. This will make your decade. Go! I'll talk to you later," Crystal says as she abruptly hangs up.

Cody sprints into the living room and turns on the television. The remote dangles from his fingers as we both watch in stunned silence as a blonde reporter announces, "In unexpected news today, District Attorney, Derek Zane, has tendered his resignation to the governor in light of charges announced by the Department of Justice."

I look over at Cody and mouth, "What charges?"

As if the reporter heard my question, she continues, "Federal officials have announced Derek Zane will be charged with racketeering, fraud, money laundering and identity theft in conjunction with his alleged activity with dog racing. Officials are being tightlipped — only confirming they have an unindicted co-conspirator and more charges will be forthcoming shortly."

The scene cuts back to the newsroom where one of the anchors asks, "What does this mean for the prosecutor's office? How will they be able to function? Does this put any of their previous cases in jeopardy?"

"Those are all excellent questions, Doug. The only answer I can give you right now is that this news has taken everyone by surprise, and no one is sure how it is all going to shake out. There is wild speculation about who the unindicted co-conspirator is — especially in light of the fact that Tori Clarkson was relieved of her duties. We have no confirmation those things are related. It's mere speculation at this point. We've reached out to the prosecutor's office for comment. Ms. Clarkson's replacement, Stacy Hildebrand, has not responded to our repeated requests."

My phone rings again and I reflexively put it up to my ear. "Did you hear that? They're just making stuff up. You're not the unindicted co-conspirator. You haven't done a single thing wrong! Did they even read the report issued by the bar? Of course not! Nobody reads that stuff except for bored lawyers. What are you going to do?" Crystal peppers me with questions. "You can't let them destroy your reputation like this."

"Crystal, my reputation was gone a long time ago. That's not the biggest issue here. I'm worried about every conviction our office has obtained since Derek Zane came on board. What is Stacy going to do about those?"

"I have no clue. Shaddick Warren came busting in the office the other day without an appointment and she left with him. She didn't come back or cancel any of her appointments. She just disappeared. It was a pain too because she was scheduled to appear in court. The judge was none too happy when we didn't have anybody there."

"Do you have anyone to cover for her?"

"No, I don't. Chelsea and Erika are in trial and they only have first-year law students as second chairs."

"Really? You're stretched that thin?"

"Yeah, I guess you haven't heard. After Derek let you go and hired Stacy, there was a mass exodus. People didn't want to work here without you."

"Wow! I wish I could help, but right now my hands are tied. Let me think about it for a bit. Right now I'm reeling from the news. I don't even know what to think. I'll call you back after I've had a chance to wrap my brain around what it means for everyone I know."

Crystal says, "I know I'm your friend — but this office doesn't run the same without you here. You should be the district attorney."

"That's sweet of you to say and I appreciate it. The reality is I don't work there anymore. Derek's legal problems don't really change that. But, let me see if I can figure out some way to help."

"I wish things were different. This shouldn't be happening to our office. The way they show us on the news is not who we are," Crystal insists tearfully.

"I know. We'll figure out some way to fix it. Hold your head up high. You are Crystal Downing,

Administrative Assistant, extraordinaire in one of the best prosecutor's offices in the country — we just have to prove people like Derek Zane and Stacy Hildebrand don't represent the heart of us."

"Okay, go do your magic. I've got to go pull myself together and pretend the universe isn't blowing up around me."

I try not to be tentative when I knock on Tristan's door, but the headquarters of Identity Bank are intimidating at best. Fortunately, this isn't the first time I've been here. Toby brought me here a couple times when we were working on building the profile of Bex Michaels and all the victims we knew of. Still, the place is enormous and classy in a way that speaks to Tristan's wealth and position.

When Tristan hears the knock on the door, he instructs me to come in. I'm surprised when I see Isaac Roguen sitting in one of the leather chairs in Tristan's office. "Tori, I'm glad you stopped by today. I imagine things are a little crazy in your life right now. I hope you don't mind, I thought my father-in-law would be helpful in this situation."

I turn to the older gentleman and introduce myself, "Hello, I'm Tori. Rogue and Ivy speak so highly of you, I feel like I already know you. Rogue tells me I should go to the gun range with you. She says you'll cure me of all my bad habits."

"Oh really? What bad habits does my daughter think I can fix?"

I blush. "Well, my job is rather high-profile — or I guess I should say my former job was high-profile. My mentor in law school suggested I become proficient with firearms. I'm not opposed — I simply have a bad habit of flinching every time I fire my weapon. Last time I went out with Jade and the twins, I was telling them how awkward I felt at the gun range and they suggested I talk to you," I confess in a rush of words.

"It certainly sounds like Rogue's instincts were right on. I'd love to take you shooting some time."

"Thank you so much. I'm sure I could use some weapons training. Although I don't think I can shoot my way out of my current problem. I hope I'm not imposing too much. The last time we were together, you said I could contact you if I needed anything. I hope you were serious," I joke as I look at Tristan.

"Guns are fun, but here at Identity Bank, we usually try to use our brains to solve problems," Tristan answers with a grin. "Seriously, if I offer my help, I intend to give it. So, what do you need?"

"Okay, just wanted to make sure I wasn't imposing."

"Tori, we've been watching the news. Impose away," Isaac instructs.

"In case you're wondering, I am not the unindicted co-conspirator. The Florida State bar cleared me of all wrongdoing. Derek Zane was after my job because I wouldn't sleep with him and probably because I went after the dog racing industry."

"We've been studying the reports Phoenix has been issuing. That man has many problems and none of them are actually you. If anything, he was probably jealous of your skills and smarts. All of his criminal enterprises don't hold a candle to your talent."

"I appreciate that, I really do. But, right now I've got two problems. The public thinks I've done something wrong —which I haven't. This puts what's left of the prosecutor's office in a position of having to defend me when they can't prove a negative. The second issue is even bigger. The person who was supposed to be replacing me is MIA and now that Derek Zane has stepped down, there isn't anyone to deal with the ramifications of his departure. It potentially puts every case he was ever part of in jeopardy. Somebody needs to be in charge of my office." I blush. "I mean my former place of employment."

Isaac studies me intently for a moment. "You were the Assistant District Attorney before you were wrongfully terminated, correct?"

I nod.

"Your standing with the bar is no longer in question?"

"I've been exonerated. They even took the inquiry off my record completely. They included a statement in their findings that Derek Zane maliciously filed a meritless complaint. The Bar Association advised me I could sue him if I wished — but I think he has enough legal problems."

"It would probably help things if the right people knew what actually happened," Tristan mutters as he writes something on a legal pad.

"It would also help if people didn't assume I was the unindicted co-conspirator, if they knew I didn't deserve to lose my job, or if they knew all those nasty things that I supposedly did in the elevator were a complete fabrication," I reply with more than a hint of sarcasm.

Tristan turns toward his father-in-law and remarks, "Well, Isaac those sound like thorough marching orders." He pivots back toward me. "Try not to worry, Tori we'll do the best we can to help you. Unfortunately, we have to go to another meeting. We'll be in touch when we have something."

Isaac clears his throat. "I have a better offer than that." He looks over at Tristan. "You forgot about the birthday party for Marcus."

"That's right. You and Cody should come. It's for Marcus, so of course there will be karaoke, but it's lots of fun. I'll have Rogue text you the details."

I grimace. "I'm not sure I'll be in much of a party mood. My life is the definition of a disaster zone right now."

"Don't you worry, *Mija*. Friday is many days away. Much can be accomplished between now and then. You just leave the fretting to us."

CHAPTER TWENTY-THREE

CODY

PAULINE, TOBY, TORI AND I are all hunched over a bank of computers in a conference room at Identity Bank trying to match the identity of nearly a dozen children and teenagers rescued during Pauline's rogue operation with the feds. No matter how hard I stare at the file in front of me and the large image on the screen, I can't make sense of it.

"Toby, I think we have a SNAFU. This file with Joey Ward's picture doesn't match. It says Christian Peña from Arizona."

Toby sets down the spreadsheet he's been working with and walks around behind me. "What's up, Cody?"

I point to the picture on the computer in front of me. "Pauline, this is who you identified as Joey Ward, right?"

"Mmm-hmm," she confirms as she pulls out a glossy print from one of her files. "I made a visual match. It's close, don't you think?"

"His hair is a little lighter, but that doesn't necessarily mean anything these days," I comment.

Toby steps up to the computer next to me and types. "Hair can be deceiving, but DNA is usually dead on." Toby nods toward his screen which brought up the same picture I was looking at before with the name Christian Peña.

"Oh, wait a second —" interrupts Pauline. "I have an idea." She rolls her chair over to Toby's computer and types with lightning speed. After a couple of seconds, a closed-circuit video of an interview appears next to his picture. It seems to be of the debriefing session with the feds. Toby's face turns pale and his hands form fists as he listens to the young man identify himself as a kidnapping victim and talk about missing his family in Colorado.

Pauline reaches out and touches Toby on his arm. "I think we've heard enough. This definitely isn't Joey Ward."

Toby glances down at her hand as if he's startled to find anyone else in the room. He looks as if he is fighting to come back from somewhere a million miles away. "We have to find this kid's family," he says gruffly.

I clear my throat. "I agree. We also have to figure out what in the heck happened to Joey Ward since this definitely isn't him."

Tori clears her throat. "I have good news on the first front. Christian's family won't be hard to track down. They are registered with the National Center for Missing and Exploited Children. They've never stopped looking for their son. They just had no idea he would end up in Florida."

"Well, technically he ended up in Alabama, but close enough," Pauline corrects.

"You didn't tell me you were in another state when

all this went down," Toby replies with a raised eyebrow.

"I'm sorry. I had to do what I had to do. I couldn't let him get away," she replies with an apologetic shrug.

"Don't apologize. I want to thank you on behalf of all the kids who were abducted who aren't able to put their thanks into words yet. Some of them may never know the risk you took and the price you'll pay. I know when I was first rescued, I was mad it took five years for people to find me. I was angry at myself for not escaping sooner. I was furious at my captor for taking me in the first place and I was livid at my parents for allowing me to be kidnapped. My reunion was not the happy event you often see on TV. It was awkward and sullen."

"I'm so sorry. You deserve to be happy," Pauline whispers through tears.

Toby stares at the monitors and blinks several times. "I am happy-*ish*. Every day it's a struggle for me to focus on who I want to be rather than what happened to me. Helping other victims of crime is one way I accomplish that."

"I admire your dedication. But still, days like this must be hard," Pauline remarks.

Toby stares down at his feet. "They are. But not as hard as sitting around doing nothing and letting evil win."

Pauline's face lights up. "Exactly! You totally get it. Now you understand why I couldn't sit back and just follow protocol. Sometimes, doing the right thing for the right reasons is more important than following the rules."

Toby nods tightly. "Sometimes — and sometimes coloring inside the lines will save your life. The trick is choosing which strategy to take."

Pauline gasps and covers her face with her hands.

"Oh my gosh, I didn't mean to sound like it was a criticism. Every situation is different."

"Like you said, this is hard for me. It pushes all sorts of buttons. I probably just misunderstood you. We should get back to working on these cases anyway," Toby replies shortly as he pulls up another picture on the computer.

Tori walks over and places her hands on Toby's shoulders and gives a reassuring squeeze. "You're doing great. This is tough work for all of us. I can't imagine putting myself in your shoes. If you need a break, let me know."

Toby smiles up at her. "Believe it or not, helping other people makes me feel stronger. Thanks for the offer though."

Pauline picks up a stack of files and walks over to stand in front of Toby. "I know we just met. But, I want you to know I think you're awesome."

"Thanks, I guess," Toby stammers. "I'm just a guy who was kidnapped as a kid who likes to do stuff on computers."

I clear my throat. "And I'm a cop who needs to go find answers about another missing kid. My gut tells me we haven't gotten straight answers. I'm going to go find Dylan so he can be the bad cop. I'll let you know if we find anything."

Tori comes over and squeezes my hands. "Cody, stay safe. Something about this situation makes me nervous."

I give Tori a brief hug. "You and me both. There is something off about this case, but I can't put my finger on it."

"Do you suppose they'll be home?" I ask as we pull up to the curb in front of the modest ranch house.

"Who knows?" Dylan answers. "How are we gonna play this? Am I the evil one this time?"

"Let's see how the chemistry works out."

"It's too bad Darya isn't here. She's always great at throwing people off kilter by being wickedly lethal."

"I kinda hope that I get to play the heavy for a change. I've been too nice lately."

"That's because love has made you dopey. You walk around with a grin on your face all the time. You're so happy I wonder if you can even be surly anymore."

"That's it. Watch me. Detective Palmer, for this operation you are now the good cop," I reply with a scowl.

Dylan shrugs. "Suits me fine, I get tired of people hating me on sight."

We walk up to the porch and knock on the door. I hear a male voice say, "Meredith, I thought you said the mail wasn't coming till this afternoon?"

"It isn't, but maybe we got those candles my sister said she'd send."

The door swings open and we come face-to-face with Mr. and Mrs. Ward. Doyle Ward almost drops his beer when he sees us. Dylan puts on a charming smile and says, "Good morning, I'm Detective Dylan Palmer. Do you mind if we come in?"

"Why would you want to do that?" Meredith Ward

asks defiantly.

"We're here to talk about Joey —" Dylan suggests as he ushers us toward the house.

Reluctantly, Doyle Ward steps aside as he mumbles, "Come on in."

I nod my appreciation. Dylan looks around and says, "Nice place you have here."

"Wanna beer?" Doyle offers as we sit down on the couch.

"Oh, no thank you," Dylan responds. "We're not allowed — you know department rules, and all."

"Mr. and Mrs. Ward, our department has been trying to reach you for quite some time. Did you not receive the messages?" I press.

"Um, we've been meaning to get back to you," Doyle responds. "We've just been busy."

"Too busy to keep in touch with the people who are looking for your lost child?" I ask skeptically. "Have you been following the news?"

"We don't watch the news much. We have Netflix now," Meredith answers.

"You're telling me that the media has been plastered with stories of recovered missing children in our area and none of your friends has bothered to call you and tell you about it? I find that hard to believe."

"We don't hang out with our friends much anymore. They don't know what to say to us since Joey went missing," Meredith hedges.

Doyle shoots his wife a look of disbelief. I turn my attention toward him. "Mr. Ward, I find it fascinating that amongst all the news reports of the children and teens which were found on the border of Florida, you never once contacted our office about the fate of your son. It's spooky, one of the children recovered is a ringer for Joey. He looks so much like your son, he had me fooled. It's almost as if you and your wife know something about where Joey is. I know if I were a parent, I would be beating the doors down at every law enforcement agency I could find. One has to wonder why you and your wife are not doing that."

Doyle shoots his wife a helpless look. "I don't know what you want me to say."

"The truth would be helpful, Mr. Ward." Dylan replies gently.

"Doyle, don't," Meredith pleads. "It all could be a big mistake. Please don't," she sobs.

"Please don't what?" Dylan probes gently. "What mistake?"

"We might as well tell them. They're not going away. They've hung around for months even though they've found nothing. Show it to them."

Robotically, Meredith gets up and walks over to the freezer. She takes out several boxes of frozen dinners, waffles and burritos. Finally she pulls out a thin Ziploc bag with what looks like a piece of mail in it. She sets it aside and methodically puts the other frozen items back in the freezer.

"I was hoping this was all a sick joke and Joey would be found with all the other missing kids. That's why I didn't tell anybody. Even my mom doesn't know about this. Doyle wouldn't have known about it either except he was digging around for ice cream a while back and I had to tell him what it was."

I look at the frosty, ice encrusted Ziploc bag and ask, "What's in the bag, Mr. Ward?"

"Joey killed himself and he wanted to make sure no one found his body. He planned it for a long time."

Meredith Ward hands me the frozen note. I gingerly try. to open it. "You believe this is a true account of what actually happened to your boy?" I press.

"I think so. Joey wanted to be a baseball player. He knew he couldn't play ball if he was blind. The cancer had come back. The doctor told him the tumor was pressing on his ocular nerve. He fought hemangiopericytoma off twice. I guess he didn't have any fight left."

"I'm so sorry. No family should have to face that. I guess what I don't understand is why you didn't tell us the whole story up front. If we would have been armed with all the facts, we could have done much more to actually help you. Instead we spent valuable resources looking in all the wrong spots," I reply, not able to hide my exasperation.

Meredith starts to shake and sob. Doyle walks over and places his arm around his wife's shoulder. "I know what she did was wrong. At first I thought Joey was just missing too. For a while, it looked like his cancer had gone into remission and he was winning. When he got the awful news again, he went into a tailspin. I don't blame him. We all did. I thought he ran off to get his head together. I figured he'd take a week or two and then go back into treatment."

Meredith picks up the story, "Joey was always so good about going to the doctor and taking his medicine. When he didn't come back, I saw the stories about the missing kids. I thought maybe that's what happened.

Then one day, I was cleaning out the fridge, and I found the note. I wanted to pretend I never found it. What mother wants to read that kind of thing? You know, Joey had brain cancer. Maybe he wasn't in his right mind when he wrote it. Maybe he didn't mean it —"

"Meredith has a point. Some of the medicine Joey took sometimes made him downright loopy."

Dylan leans forward. "This is a lot of new information that we didn't have before. Would you mind coming down to the station, so we can re-interview you while we have our computers and maps available? There are a lot of scenarios we need to look at in light of these new developments."

"Is my wife going to be in trouble for what she did?"

"We are not the ones who make those kind of calls, Mr. and Mrs. Ward. That's way above our pay grade. We're just searching for your son and hundreds of other missing people every year. We can only do that job effectively if we have the whole story," I explain.

Doyle looks at his wife. "Meredith, it's the least we can do. We owe it to Joey either way."

She sobs. "I'm afraid of the answer."

Dylan pats her on the shoulder. "I know it's hard. But not knowing is excruciating too, right?"

"Every minute he's gone feels like a decade."

"I imagine so. Let's put all the cards on the table and figure out where we stand. It's the only way Officer Erickson and I can truly help."

CHAPTER TWENTY-FOUR

TORI

I SMOOTH OUT AN almost invisible wrinkle in my suit as I look in the mirror. It's been almost a full year since I made closing arguments wearing this suit. I spin around and wobble on my high heels as I face Cody. "Do you know why I've been summoned to Derek's old office?"

He tenderly kisses me on the forehead. "I don't — but you look amazing. Maybe they need your help to go through some of his old files? After all, they haven't been able to find Stacy Hildabrand. They might need you for institutional memory."

"Wouldn't they just use Crystal Downing? She's got more institutional memory than the rest of us combined. Truth be told, it doesn't matter who is at the head of the office, Crystal is the true heart."

"That's not how I hear it. Everyone I've spoken to said the office lost its heart when you left."

I smile. "You're so sweet. I believe you're supposed to say that because you're my boyfriend. I'll figure it out when I get there I suppose — I just hate to go into these things blind."

"Tori, I think you have forgotten how masterful you are at thinking on your feet. Whatever this is, you've got this handled."

"I hope you're right. Life has been throwing us some pretty tough curveballs lately."

Cody helps me put my coat on and kisses my neck. "True enough. But, I'd like to think there have been some phenomenal ones too."

I don't know what I expected coming back to Derek Zane's old stomping grounds, but this wasn't it. Oh, the office is still completely ostentatious and not at all what I'm used to as a prosecutor, but all traces of my former supervisor have been removed. It looks less like a swanky bachelor pad and much more like a traditional upscale law office. After a nervous temporary receptionist escorts Cody and I back to what used to be Derek's office, I'm surprised when the assistant to the lieutenant governor joins us. Cody immediately stands up to shake her hand. "Susan! I didn't expect to see you here today."

She smiles awkwardly. "Honestly, I expected to have a little company. But my boss and his boss got called away on an emergency. So … you'll have to get the news from me. I hope you don't mind."

Susan shakes my hand too and then sits in one of the large, imposing leather chairs. After a few moments, I try to break the tension. "Since I wasn't expecting to receive any news today, I guess I don't care who delivers it to me — unless of course it's bad news. Then it would suck to be you," I finish with a laugh.

Susan's brows furrow. "Well, I don't think this is bad news. I suppose you could have moved on with your life in the last few months … I guess I won't know until I ask, will I?"

"You're making me a little nervous here," I confess.

"I'll just get right to it then —" Susan says as she clears her throat.

Cody leans forward and puts his arm around my waist as we sit on the edge of our seats.

"As I said, the lieutenant governor and the governor had hoped to be here today. In part to apologize for what our state has put you through during the last year. As you know, your departure from the prosecutor's office has left a big hole. By all accounts, you were a very effective Assistant District Attorney. It is a shame someone's pettiness and political ambitions were put ahead of the public good. We would like to try to reverse some of the damage starting today. The governor would like to appoint you to the District Attorney position vacated by Derek Zane."

My breath catches in my throat. Cody's hand trembles against my back. When I can finally speak, I ask, "I don't understand. There was someone hired in my position. I don't work for the county anymore. I was fired and as far as I know, no one has reinstated me. Stacy Hildebrand would be next in line."

"The governor considered Ms. Hildebrand. To put it mildly, he was not impressed with her credentials. He was baffled by her initial appointment. By all appearances, she didn't meet the minimum qualifications of the job."

Cody clears his throat as he chokes back a laugh. "She admitted as much to me. She stated it was all about using her connections to get the position."

Susan nods. "Apparently, those connections were also her downfall. She seems to be on the run after being named an unindicted co-conspirator with Mr. Zane and Councilman Warren."

I can't help myself. I laugh out loud. "Hardly the qualities you want in the District Attorney. This is surreal. They tried to pin a bunch of bogus unethical behavior on me when they were the ones basically running a crime ring."

"Exactly. The governor wants someone who is familiar with the operations of the office. Someone the staff trusts to help rebuild the reputation. That person is you. So, Victoria Clarkson, do you accept the position?"

I look over at Cody with my eyes wide open in shock. "Did you know this would happen?"

Cody shrugs. "Not specifically. But you totally deserve it."

"I don't know. It's a lot of responsibility. There are still plenty of people who believe I did what I was accused of doing. I don't know if they'll accept me in a leadership position," I reply as thoughts whirl in my head.

"There might be a few naysayers — that's true. But, your former boss, the councilman, and who knows who else will go to trial soon. The truth will come out. The person hired to replace you was basically unqualified and just put in the position as a political favor. No one knows for sure all of Derek Zane's reasons for terminating you — but the obvious ones have to do with retaliation for your win in the puppy mill case and flat out sexual harassment. Most of the people who have worked with you for years will understand the truth once they hear all the facts," Cody argues.

"Not only that, when the Governor makes the formal appointment, he will be abundantly careful to lay out all of your stellar qualifications and put to rest any remaining doubts about you," Susan adds.

I swallow hard. "Do you mind if I take time to think about this? On one hand, it's everything I've wanted and worked toward for years. Yet, it still feels as if it's too good to be true. I need to evaluate whether I'm able to take this on given a few challenges in my personal life."

Susan chews on her bottom lip. "I suppose. We'd like to get this wrapped up as soon as possible. The office has been in disarray for quite some time. The sooner we can get it all settled, the better. But, I understand this offer came out of the blue and it's a major upheaval in your life. Please consider it as quickly as possible and get back to me as soon as you can." Susan bends down and digs through her briefcase and pulls out a business card. She flips it over and writes a number on the back. "This is my cell number. You can call any time, day or night, to let me know your decision. I know the governor will be anxiously awaiting any news. I want you to make the best decision for you, but I also want to be a little selfish here and let you know that personally, I hope you choose to take the job. My daughter is in law school right now. I hope she grows up to be the kind of attorney you are."

I stand up, walk over, and take the card from her. "Thank you so much, Susan. I don't mean to put you in an awkward situation with your boss. I'm sure they hoped I would jump at the chance for a promotion. It's just that my life is so chaotic right now. I feel like I need to take a moment to catch my breath before I close my eyes and leap. I don't want to make the wrong choice simply because it feels good for my ego."

"I understand. I've been at many of those crossroads in my career. Like I said, call me day or night. I wish the governor would've been here, he is much more persuasive than me," Susan says as she gathers up her belongings.

I touch her on the shoulder to stop her. "Susan, your presentation was perfect. I appreciate your honesty. It's just my life is super complicated right now. I'll let you know."

Cody walks up behind me and grasps my hand and gives it a squeeze as he whispers in my ear. "Don't worry, we'll figure this out."

I'm trying not to spill anything as I try to clear room on my crowded dining room table. "Mom, are you sure you don't want more meatloaf?"

"No, I'm fine. Your young man said you made some pie. I should save room."

"I did. Would you like it now or later?"

My mom sighs and shifts in her wheelchair. "I appreciate the dinner, but I'm getting tired. Besides, you look sad. Are you breaking up with your boyfriend?"

I'm a taken aback by my mom's abrupt change of topic. "No, Mom — Cody and I are great. You can ask him. He's sitting right here."

"Mrs. Clarkson, I love your daughter very much. Why would you think otherwise?" Cody asks.

"I told you to call me Velma. You two look like you're

about to rob a bank you're so tense. Did you hear bad news from my doctors or something?"

I blow out a breath of relief. "No, Mom, that's not it at all. This time it has nothing to do with you. The doctors say you're doing great. In fact, your hip is doing well enough we can talk about moving you home, if you'd like."

"I don't want to move. I like the nurses there. There's someone there all the time, and I have friends. Sometimes when I don't feel so good, it's good to have the doctors there too. I don't want to fall down and get hurt again."

I'm not sure whether I feel more disappointed or relieved. On days like today when my mom is so lucid she seems like her old self, it's difficult to remember the awful days when she is a danger to herself and everyone else. Although I was hopeful the new treatment would be permanently helpful, it seems to be cyclical at best. I smile gamely. "You're right, Mom. The facility you're in takes really great care of you. I'm just worried about other things. I was offered a new job and I am scared I might not be ready to take it."

"Why not?" my mom demands with a shrewd look. "You've always been the smartest girl I know." She turns to Cody. "Don't you agree?"

Cody nods. "I do. Tori has just been beaten up by the press and a few coworkers recently. Her faith in herself is a little shaken."

My mom looks befuddled. "Well that's stupid. I may be losing my marbles to some dumb disease, but even I know my daughter is bright and talented. If they have something bad to say about her, they're wrong. If she was offered a new job, she should just take it."

Cody stands up and walks over to give my mom a hug. "Velma, you don't know this, but Tori was just telling me today as we were fixing dinner how much she wished she could get your advice about what to do. Thank you for sharing your opinion. I think it will make her decision much easier."

I wipe away tears as I announce. "It does, Mom. Guess what? I'm going to be the District Attorney."

"I always knew you were destined for greatness. I just wish your daddy would have lived long enough to see this."

"Me too. I know he would've been so proud of me."

Epilogue

Cody

Tori tosses me the keys to her new rig and winks. "I guess I trust you to drive the beast."

"Have I told you how much I love your new ride?"

Tori grins. "I figured after all those hellaciously long hours at the office, I deserved to treat myself. Besides, your Mustang isn't designed to deal with all the trips we take to the beach. I decided a four-wheel-drive would be a better choice."

I hop in the driver's seat and throw on my sunglasses. I lean over and kiss Tori deeply. I take a moment to kiss the crook of her neck after I pull away. "Happy anniversary to us! Can you believe it's been a year since we went on our first date?"

"I don't know how to answer your question. In some ways, it seems way less than a year. In other ways, it seems like ten years. We've crammed every possible crisis into just a few short months."

"At least we don't have to face a trial for Bex Michaels and his wife. They both pled guilty. All those kids won't have to testify."

"Have you spoken to any of them recently?" Tori asks me.

"Yeah, actually I have. DeAndre has actually followed through on his promise to pursue a career in law enforcement. He has joined the junior officer program and has a mentor with our department."

"That's awesome. Have you heard how the others are doing?"

"Isadora is having the toughest time. She was really attached to Bex's children. They adore her too. So, the counselor is working on a plan with the family to see if there can be some sort of contact between them."

"That would be nice. It had to be traumatic for all of them."

"Tallulah is headed to college on scholarship if her parents will allow it after all she's been through."

"Any breakthrough on Joey Ward?"

"Nothing so far. Pauline and Toby have been pouring over every lead. So far, nothing has panned out. They're even working with Phoenix. But so far, they haven't cracked the code."

"That has to be devastating for his parents."

"It is. I still get frustrated every time I think about it. What would've happened if they would've told us the truth from the beginning? We lost weeks and months of valuable search time chasing inaccurate leads because they didn't tell us the truth."

Tori reaches out and grabs my hand. "I know, that must be incredibly demoralizing."

I pull the SUV out into traffic as I shrug

philosophically. "Unfortunately, I can't turn back time and re-create evidence. So, we're doing the best we can."

"I know, but it still sucks. I know you wanted to solve this case a long time ago."

I pass a couple of slow trucks and then go back into the slow lane. "Speaking of things which suck, how are things going at the office?"

"Well, it wasn't quite as bad as I had envisioned. I guess we're fortunate Derek wasn't intricately involved in the day-to-day operation of our office even though he said he was. He actually did very little work for someone whose title was District Attorney. It's frustrating, but in this case, it helped us a lot. His impact on former cases is minimal."

I grimace. "I'm not sure if I should cheer about the news or be thoroughly disgusted."

Tori bursts out laughing. "Oh trust me, I have the same conversation with myself every single day. Thank goodness for Crystal, she keeps me sane."

Tori's stomach growls audibly. "I see you're looking forward to our date at the crab shack is much as I am," I joke.

Just as we pull up to the crab shack, my cell phone rings. It's Dylan's ring tone. I look over at Tori with a thunderous expression, my disappointment clear. She motions for me to answer the phone.

"This better be good," I growl at my former partner. "It's my anniversary! You know I have special plans tonight —"

As I listen to what Dylan says on the other end of the phone, the blood drains out of my face and I start to feel a little dizzy.

Tori notices and hands me my soda. "Are you okay?" she whispers.

I shake my head as I listen to Dylan.

"Are they sure? There's a DNA match? In Minnesota? Crap!"

Tori squeezes my hand and lays her head against my shoulder in a show of support.

I scrub my hand down my face. "All right, I don't know if I can do anything about it now, but I'll talk to Tori and get back to you."

I blink back tears as I hang up my phone and stick it back in my pocket.

Somberly, I turn to Tori. "Well, our string remains unbroken. This is our third attempt at a date at the crab shack, and this is the third time we've been interrupted by one of my cases."

Tori simply holds me tighter. "Who did they find?"

"Joey Ward. They found his body a few months ago, but he was labeled as a John Doe. He was so emaciated by the cancer, they couldn't determine his proper age and he had no ID. He was found in an old fishing shack on one of the lakes in Minnesota. Until we expanded the search, no one knew we were looking for him."

"You need to be the one to tell Meredith and Doyle. They trust you. Don't make Dylan do this. He's been through enough on this case."

I lean back against the headrest and close my eyes. "This is not how I planned this date. I was going to ask you to marry me. There's a ring in my pocket."

"If you would've asked me, I would've said yes — because you are the best thing that's ever happened to me.

You proved to me that love triumphs over injustice even under the harshest conditions. So, maybe tonight wasn't the perfect night for a proposal. Yet, in a way it was."

I look at Tori as if she's lost her ever lovin' mind.

She just smiles softly. "We're two people who love each other and our jobs. Sometimes, our priorities will collide with each other. But we're stronger people because of who we are and what we do."

I shift in the car and pull out the ring. "Just so you know, I had something much more romantic planned. But you took the words right out of my mouth. Victoria Clarkson, will you marry me?"

"In a heartbeat, Cody DeWayne Erickson. Our timing might be weird, but it works for us. I love you."

THE END (for now…)

Note from the Author

Dear Reader,

Thanks for reading my book. If you enjoyed reading about people who are not so stereotypical, then I've got good news…

… there's more.

He's always been passionate about his work, but not this way.

Detective Palmer has become known for his dedication to finding missing children. Now he's been asked to form a special cold case unit.

His first assignment may be his toughest.

His mom wants him to find the daughter of an old family friend.

But there are complications he never expected.

He's never had to put his emotions before his job.

What happens when love hits out of thin air?

Out of Thin Air is available now in paperback, Kindle and Kindle Unlimited.

~Mary

Because love matters, differences don't.

ACKNOWLEDGMENTS

Cody has always been one of my favorite characters since I introduced him way back in *Pieces*. He is unique guy — tough and hardened by his job, yet tender and funny. I knew he would need a strong woman who wouldn't be afraid to push back a little against his macho tendencies.

A lot of romances (mine included) often feature one character giving up their career to help another character succeed. Sometimes that can happen in real life. Yet more often than not, couples are left to try to negotiate a balance between their careers and their family lives. I thought it would be a great theme to show the stresses of modern family life juxtaposed against fighting for successful careers. I love this story because Tori and Cody are great cheerleaders for each other.

I have lots of great cheerleaders in my life too. Honestly, I couldn't do what I do without the support of my husband and my children. I keep absolutely crazy hours as an author. My husband and my son, Justin, do a great job of keeping the real world running while I'm lost in the world of fiction. Left to my own devices, I would probably starve.

I'd like to give a shout out to my personal assistant, LJ Redding, who keeps things running smoothly behind-the-scenes.

Kathy Faltinson, thanks for taking the reins and being the editor on this one. We all know sometimes it's hard to make sense of my words.

Thanks as always to my research assistant and beta reader, Kathern Watts.

Kudos to my proofreaders, Justin Crawford, Lisa Lee and Christina Bergmann.

 Huge cyber hugs to all my fans who have stayed loyal to these characters and are always curious about what they are up to next. It is because of you I continue to have a job. Thank you for supporting books that celebrate diversity.

ABOUT THE AUTHOR

I HAVE BEEN LUCKY enough to live my own version of a romance novel. I married the guy who kissed me at summer camp. He told me on the night we met that he was going to marry me and be the father of my children.

Eventually, I stopped giggling when he said it, and we've been married for more than thirty years. We have two children. The oldest is a Doctor of Osteopathy. He is across the United States completing his residency, but when he's done, he is going to come back to Oregon and practice Family Medicine. Our youngest son is now tackling high school and where he is an honor student. He is interested in becoming an EMT.

I write full time now. I have published more than thirty books and have several more underway. I volunteer my time to a variety of causes. I have worked as a Civil Rights Attorney and diversity advocate. I spent several years working for various social service agencies before becoming an attorney.

In my spare time, I love to cook, decorate cakes and of course, I obsessively, compulsively read.

I would be honored if you would take a few moments out of your busy day to check out my website, MaryCrawfordAuthor.com. While you're there, you can sign up for my newsletter and get a free book. I will be announcing my upcoming books and giving sneak peeks as well as sponsoring giveaways and giving you information about other interesting events.

If you have questions or comments, please E-mail me at Mary@MaryCrawfordAuthor.com or find me on the following social networks:

Facebook: www.facebook.com/authormarycrawford

Website: MaryCrawfordAuthor.com

Twitter: www.twitter.com/MaryCrawfordAut

www.ingramcontent.com/pod-product-compliance
Lightning Source LLC
Chambersburg PA
CBHW051302210726
48287CB00002B/635